Unleashing Hell

The Complete Collection

VIOLA TEMPEST

Unleashing Hell

The Complete Collection

Cover Design by Mayflower Studio
Website: www.mayflowerstudio.com

CONTENTS

UNLEASHING HELL BOOK ONE

FINDING HIM

VIOLA TEMPEST

CHAPTER 1

My name is Bella Nova, and my family and I just moved from Astoria, Oregon to Ojai, California. Why? Because six months ago, I killed someone. Now, before you start judging me, calling me names like a "monster" or a "criminal," know that it wasn't my fault. Turned out, shooting someone in the name of self-defense isn't legal in all counties, and I had to find out the hard way.

But let me take a few steps back. I'm just your

normal average seventeen-year-old high school student, nothing more, nothing less. I went to school, got good grades, hung out with my friends, and on weekends, I volunteered at the local animal shelter, where I fed and groomed the animals, preparing them for their new home. All in all, I was the good child, the one who followed all the rules and did as I was told. Unlike my brother, Ace, who ran with all the potheads and stayed out for days at a time.

So, how did I end up in the back of a man's pickup truck? Bound and tied like a chicken ready to be chopped and served? Let's just say, I'm not exactly the smartest grape in the bunch. I excelled when it came to exams and standardized tests, but in the outside world, in reality, my intense lust for any guy who bats his eyes at me, and dreadful fear of ending up alone, usually put me in positions I shouldn't be in.

And Brick Cannon was just too delicious to resist. He came into my high school like a blazing fire, captivating the hearts of everyone he encountered, everyone except for me. And I hated it! I'd watch with envy as he flirted with my best friend, Chelsea Miller, and it drove me insane whenever he'd just brush right past me to get to her. Like I didn't even exist!

I resented Chelsea for it. Though it wasn't her fault, it also didn't help that she flirted back with him whenever she got the chance, much like all the other girls in my school. He was the most handsome boy I had ever seen in my life, and I'm sure they all thought the same.

But then my luck started to change. Whenever I'd turn around, I'd catch Brick staring at me for a quick second before turning his head away. Was he really looking at me? Or were those eyes just for Chelsea? I second guessed myself for weeks, assuming a boy like him would never be with a girl like me, until he came up to me one day as I was walking home.

"Hey, Bella," he said, flashing me that charming smile, enough to make me swoon. "Whatcha up to?"

I froze. Of course, I did. I'd never spoken to Brick before, always lusting after him from afar, so when he finally came up to me, I didn't know what else to do.

"Hey...," I answered back. "Um, Chelsea isn't here."

He laughed, so heartily that I was sure the entire neighborhood heard.

"Chelsea?" he exclaimed. "Forget about her. It's you I wanna talk to, silly."

My mouth hung open as I pointed to myself. "Me?"

I wasn't sure whether to cheer or faint. After all this time, Brick Cannon, *the* Brick Cannon, actually wanted to talk to me!

"Of course! Why'd you think I hung around Chelsea so much? Because I was too scared to talk to you."

My eyes lit up. I couldn't believe what I was hearing. It was everything I'd always wanted, and I wanted, right then and there, to leap up and throw my arms around his neck.

Brick Cannon. He was interested in me. And I couldn't ask for more.

But although Brick was the greatest, he was definitely not my first... crush, that is. Before my parents met, my mother used to be a bit of a... promiscuous damsel, hitting up clubs every night and bringing home a different boy. I've heard all the stories of her wild teenage years. So have the rest of my family, each one less enthusiastic about my mother's sexuality than I was.

GROWING UP, I told myself that I would never end up like her, that I would meet the one man of my dreams, get married, and that was it. And I held myself to that promise, until I entered middle school. And everything changed. I had hit puberty and became a woman, and I instantly became hooked on every troublemaker who crossed my path.

At first, it was Billy Styles, my sixth-grade crush whom everyone wanted, and he knew it. It amazed me how much of an ego was able to fit inside such a small package. The girls in my class were just getting over their "cooties" stage, and they all threw themselves at the new "bad boy" who had recently enrolled in our school. And I was no different.

Of course, like all the boys during that time, Billy

wanted nothing to do with any of us. Video games and soccer were his calling, not dating, and that only made us all want him that much more.

But that obsession quickly faded when Alex Shaw came into my life two years later. His blonde hair and beautiful blue eyes were enough to make me shiver in all the right places. I wanted nothing more than to be his girlfriend, to lock my arm around his as we stroll to class together.

Unfortunately, his eyes were on Becky Miller, the most popular girl in class, and the one all the boys wanted to date. I didn't stand a chance. I watched in the shadows as Alex and Becky locked their arms together and walked by me every day down the hall. And whenever they kissed, their lips locking and tongues intertwining, I wanted to puke.

I wasn't ugly, per se. I just didn't have *the* look that boys seemed to want. I was just your average girl next door with high standards. I had plenty of suitors knocking on my door, but I wanted the best of the best, the cream of the crop, and I wasn't about to settle for anything less. I'd rather be alone than stoop myself to such level.

Lucky enough for me, Becky Miller's father eventually received an offer he couldn't refuse, and moved his entire family to Chicago, Illinois, forcing Alex and Becky to break up. I smirked as I watched them break it off, making promises to continue their relationship long distant even though everyone knew it wouldn't last, and Alex was in tears as he watched Becky hop in her dad's car and drive away.

And I was right. Less than a week later, Alex turned into a wreck when he saw a picture of his girlfriend on social media with another guy, smiling and laughing as if Alex didn't exist. And guess who was right there to comfort him? Me. No one ever told me that the best time to snag a man is during his lowest point, but that's exactly how I became Alex Shaw's new girlfriend just days later.

We did everything that he and Becky used to do, locking arms as we walked to class, and locking lips while our tongues entangled in a dance. After two months of dating, we even made love for the first time. I'd felt nervous at first, reserved and shy, but he managed to convince me that, if I really loved him, I had to do it for him.

And so, I did, letting my sexual fantasies run wild as he claimed my virginity for himself. I finally had everything I'd ever wanted, and it felt magical.

But maybe all that lust and desire clouded my judgment, because soon, I began to realize that Alex Shaw wasn't who I thought he was. Not at all.

It was our Sophomore year in high school when I finally discovered that my boyfriend had been cheating on me the entire time of our relationship. He had started dating Virginia Wilde soon after Becky left, and was only with me because Virginia refused to put out. "The Middle School Slut," I was known as, and I wanted to die when I found out, overhearing a conversation that Alex was having with his group of friends, bragging about how he'd had sex over thirty-six times.

And I couldn't take it anymore. It was too much. Everywhere I went, guys came up to me, asking me to fuck them, and girls all avoided me, thinking that I'd somehow spread whatever disease I had to them. I felt so alone, so suicidal, that I convinced my parents to transfer me to a new school, in a different county, where no one knew who I was or my past. And that's where I met Brick.

"You like me?" I asked before realizing how awkward and stupid I probably sounded.

All he said was that he wanted to talk to me, and here I was throwing myself at him and expecting something much more.

But he didn't laugh. He didn't point his finger at me and call me an "idiot" like I had expected.

Instead, he rubbed the back of his neck and nodded. "Yeah, I kinda do. Do you maybe wanna grab a soda with me? And it can just be as friends! I don't want to pressure you into anything you're uncomfortable with."

I quickly nodded. "As friends," I said.

I couldn't have him knowing that those few words had already made my panties wet, and I wanted to just tear his clothes off and lick those abs that I imagined he had.

I barely got to know Brick during our date. I was too busy staring into his beautiful eyes, and he was too busy running his fingers up and down my inner thigh. We both wanted each other. Not just as boyfriend and girlfriend, but we both wanted to grab each other by the shirt and make out right then and there in the booth of the diner. And it became much more obvious when he leaned in and kissed me, running his hand up the skirt of my dress and pulling down my cheeky.

"Wait! Not here," I hissed. "There are people here."

Brick looked around and saw three elders slurping on their bowl of soup. Probably all here for the early bird special. His face fell when he tried to persuade me again but was stopped instead.

"I know somewhere we can go. It's old, abandoned, and no one will be there to bother us," he whispered into my ear while nibbling on it.

I eagerly agreed, and he took my hand and led me into his pickup truck. I hesitated and winced when his hand made its way down my underwear, but I really wanted him to like me, so I didn't stop his fingers from exploring. I could feel my body falling for his touch, his sensual touch that made me the wettest I'd ever been. He eventually stopped in front of an old barn that looked like it hadn't been touched in nearly a century and asked me if the place was fine.

But my body had already caved in, and I couldn't

even make it out the door of the car before climbing on top of him and unzipping his pants, feeling the girth of him inside of me while I smashed my face against his.

OUR WILD SEXUAL adventure continued for months, fucking everywhere we could, whenever we could, and I had become so head over heels in love with him that I threw all my reserves and common sense right out the window.

Chelsea tried to warn me about Brick, but I refused to listen.

"He's not a good person," she said. "Why do you think I stopped talking to him? All he wants is sex, controlling and manipulating women into giving him what he wants. Don't you see it? Doesn't it seem odd to you that he only ever wants to be around you if you put out?"

But I just rolled my eyes at her. Chelsea had been my best friend ever since I transfer to Astoria High, but there was no chance in Hell that I was going to let her come between me and the boy of my dreams.

"You're just jealous that he wants me and not you. Brick loves me," I said back to her. "I love him, and we're going to be together forever."

I should've listened to Chelsea when I had the chance. Even my mother, the Queen of Lust, tried to warn me about Brick Cannon. There was a certain sense of evil in his eyes that I'd failed to notice until it was too late.

He had killed before, he told me when I ultimately found myself being held captive in that abandoned barn. And I wouldn't be his last, just another pawn to satisfy his craving as he made his way across the country. And here I was thinking Alex Shaw was bad. Never did I imagine being manipulated and kidnapped by a fucking serial killer.

And that's how I ended up in California. On the run for shooting a man before he had a chance to shoot me first. They may come after me. After all, I *had* committed a crime. But they might not. I had played the role of a vigilante, and shooting Brick Cannon only meant sparing the lives of many other women he had planned on conquering.

I could sit here and think about all the possibilities of my fate, but I'd much rather tune them all out and forget about my past. I have a new life now in Ojai, and though it seems like I'm always running from one problem to another, these were all life-or-death situations. I had no other choice.

CHAPTER 2

Ojai, California is a small valley just north of Los Angeles, where people are both friendly and superstitious. Although they'd do anything, even things out of their way, to help a newcomer settle in and make this town their home, they'd never refrain from telling their own tales of how Ojai is haunted. No one knows why or what it's haunted by; they just know that once every thousand years, something strange happens to the town of Ojai, a sort of vibration, followed by an aura that many of the elders deem as "evil."

Some of the more superstitious folks think it's a sign from God, his way of warning the residents that the end is near and to get their shit together before the whole world collapses. Others just brush it off as another earthquake, something that's common to residents of California, given how it resides on the San Andreas Fault.

But whatever it is, no one has ever lived long enough after the incident to carry on the message. Maybe the world really does end once every thousand years. Maybe God does open the Gate of Heaven and sends the good ones up. Or maybe, everyone in this town is full of nonsense and bullshit.

"You folks better be careful," one of our neighbors warns us as my father pulls into the driveway of our new home. "It's another thousand years again. Who knows what, or who, will come upon us this year? My husband, Charlie, and I have been preparing for over a year now."

"Preparing?" my mother asks, pulling a suitcase from the trunk.

"For the apocalypse!"

That's when the husband walks out. "Oh, don't listen to Betsy. It's all just nonsense. There's no apocalypse. It's just a little vibration, nothing to be too concerned about."

"But we do have that bomb shelter, you know, just in case." Betsy points out to Charlie.

"That's true, we do. I doubt we'll need it, but it never hurts to have a backup."

"Thanks for the heads up," my father says as he walks into the home.

"Anytime, neighbors!" Betsy calls out after him. "And if you folks need a place to stay during the apocalypse, our shelter has plenty of room!"

"It's not an apocalypse, Betsy!" Charlie angrily storms inside and slams the door behind him.

Betsy turns to the rest of us and apologizes. "Oh, don't mind him. Charlie's always cranky in the morning, but you'll get used to him. Anyway, welcome to Ojai, and be safe out there. If the apocalypse doesn't kill us, some of the weirdos who cross through here from LA most likely will. It's a dangerous, dangerous world." She finishes and proceeds to walk back into her home.

"Is there really an apocalypse coming?" Ace asks our parents, plopping his ass down on the couch, still wrapped and sealed.

"Nah," my father says. "Don't mind them. They're old. They don't know what they're talking about. An apocalypse every thousand years? A sign from God? Come on, it's all a bunch of rumors. Probably to scare away newcomers." He sits down beside Ace. "Ojai's a great town. I've heard nothing but good things about this place. Don't let our crazy neighbors get to you."

"Your father's right, kids. Nothing's going to happen. The apocalypse is nothing but a rumor. Now, go set up your rooms. You both start school tomorrow," Mom chimes in.

I pick up my bags and head up to my room. The stairs creak as I walk, and the flimsy railing makes me wonder whether I'm safer skipping it altogether. The house is old, a Victorian-style home, probably from the early 1800s. It smells of dust and old people, and I wouldn't be surprised if I find several rats living up in the attic.

Ace had already claimed his room by the time I make my way upstairs, belly flopped on his floor mattress while playing on his phone. I have no choice but to choose the other one, the smaller, much smaller, bedroom. It's always the same wherever we go. Ace would get the better option. Perks of being the older one, I guess.

I never liked change, but this is one I desperately needed. I can't go back to Astoria. Too much history back there that I'd rather forget. And Chelsea, I never got the chance to tell her that I was moving. But it wasn't like we'd really spoken since I ignored her for Brick. I sigh. That's my life, always making bad choices and screwing everything up.

After throwing my suitcase onto the carpeted floor, I walk over to the windowsill, twisting the pentagram ring on my right ring finger. Brick had given it to me on our third date, said it suited my style, and for me to cherish it forever. Now, I keep thinking whether he just swiped it off a dead girl. But still, it holds sentimental value. I think I'll keep it for now.

The wind is blowing heavily outside, splatters of rain whacking hard against the pane. I look outside, and even amid the gloomy and depressing weather, the townspeople don't seem to mind. Yellow coats and purple umbrellas line the streets, and cars slowly glide along the roads as if no one is ever in a rush.

"Bella! Ace!" I hear my mother cry out. "Time for lunch!"

I spin around to head back downstairs. I can always unpack later. The day is long, and the night is longer. There's really no point in rushing. Besides, I could hear my stomach growl the entire ride down. I need to eat something before I pass out.

When I walked into the kitchen, Mom's already setting the table with plates of turkey and brie sandwiches for everyone, with a large bowl of tomato soup sitting in the center.

"Juice?" she asks me as I sit down.

"No, thanks. I'll just have some water." I reach over in front of me and pour myself a glass.

"Pour me some of that, will ya?"

I look up, and Ace walks in, sitting himself down also, phone still in hand. I roll my eyes at him, but he doesn't seem to notice. Hell, he never seems to notice.

"Take mine," I respond, handing the glass over to him before returning to pour myself another. "Where's Dad?" I ask Mom.

"Unloading the rest of the trunk. He'll be in soon."

I watch as Mom finishes wiping her hands on a towel and grabs a few utensils from the drawer.

Such a motherly figure. It's hard to believe that she once worked in a strip club.

"So," Mom asks after taking a few bites of her sandwich. "You two ready for your first day of school?"

"Why do I have to go to the same school as Bella here, anyway?" Ace whines. "She'll just embarrass me. No one wants to be seen with their kid sister."

"Hey! You're no prize, either!" I retort.

"Stop it!" Dad throws his sandwich on his plate and interjects. "We've talked about this. Villanova Prep is the best school in the area. And your mother and I want you both to have the best education we can afford. So, unless you want to end up on the streets of LA with all the addicts on Skid Row, I suggest you keep your mouth shut and enjoy what you're given."

"What's wrong, Bella?" Mom asks when she notices me picking at my sandwich instead of eating it.

I shrug, and even though I'm trying to focus on Mom, I can still hear my father and Ace bickering beside me.

"What if nothing changes? It's a new school, a new town, but what if my past comes back to haunt me? What if I fall for another guy who ruins me?"

Mom places her sandwich back on her plate and comes over to sit beside me. She wraps her arms around mine and pulls me in for a hug.

"Remember what we talked about, honey. Whatever happened in the past, stays in the past. Learn from it. Grow from it. I trust that things will be different for you this time. We left Astoria for a reason, so you can start over. Don't let it all be for nothing."

"Yeah," Ace yells over. "Don't kill anyone this time."

My face immediately turns red, and all the pain I had tried so hard to suppress comes rushing back. I push my chair back and throw the rest of my sandwich at him. "You jerk!"

Tears continue to pour from my eyes as I run upstairs into my room and slam the door. I can hear my mom scolding him for what he had said, but the tears won't stop flowing.

I'm a monster. A murderer. A slut. All that and more that I will never be able to truly escape from.

CHAPTER 3

The next morning, my alarm blares before the sun's even out. I wake up with tired eyes and a pounding headache. I had tossed and turned all night, the flashbacks of my past creeping into my nightmare. Sometimes when I sleep, I can still see the stains of Brick's blood on my hands, the life of another person gone because of me. It's a blemish that will forever be part of my record, a brand that I can never run from no matter what I end up accomplishing.

How could someone so handsome, so charming, so sexy, turn out to be such a monster? I'll also always wonder how our relationship would've turned out if he didn't turn out to be a serial killer. Three kids, twin girls and one boy, a small cottage in the woods with a small pond behind it. That's how I would've liked that relationship to have turned out.

Brick Cannon was my greatest love, a wild adventure I'll never forget, and even though he ultimately died by my own hands, he'll always have a special place in my heart, the gold standard for every boy who comes after him.

I glance over at the uniform laying on my bed, a white button-down blouse, a blue plaid mini skirt, and blue and white saddle shoes, topped with matching knee-length socks. I sigh again. I never had to wear a uniform before, but maybe this is better. Maybe forcing everyone to dress the same will prevent some girls from getting all the hot guys. I quickly shake my head at that thought. No, that can't be my focus. Not anymore. It's done nothing but get me into trouble.

As I strip off my pajamas, letting it all fall to the floor, I can't help but stare at the scar on my left arm, my mind flashing back again. Brick had left it when his nails clawed into me while I tried to escape, ripping into my flesh and pulling me back. The excruciating pain was too much to bear, but I knew I had to keep pulling away if I wanted even a slim chance of getting away. It hadn't quite healed properly, a constant reminder of my dangerous rendezvous with love, but somehow, I preferred it this way.

The blue plaid skirt didn't quite reach the length I had wanted it to when I pulled it on. I can still see the bite marks left on my inner thigh from when Brick nibbled on them after going down on me during one of our passionate affairs. They were innocent at first. "Love bites" as I call them. But then he got rough, aggressive, and now, I have three sets of teeth marks imprinted onto my skin.

After pulling on my socks, I walk over to my vanity and grab my concealer. It's the best thing I can think of with such last-minute notice. But still, despite how much of the cream I plaster on, I can still see the faint marks sitting there, mocking me.

"Bella! You ready up there? We're gonna miss the bus!" Ace calls up from the living room.

Fuck. I get up and quickly grab my backpack from my closet. It's filled with nothing but a couple pencils and a small notebook, but what else am I supposed to bring with me on my first day of school? I then quickly climb into my shoes, grab my phone, and hurry down the stairs, where I find Ace standing there with his arms crossed over his chest.

"About time," he huffs.

I mumble "sorry" and follow him out the door to the bus stop, which is only a few feet from our house.

"You better stay away from me at school," Ace

mutters in my direction. "There, we're complete strangers. Got it? There, you're not my kid sister."

"Stop calling me a kid! And fine, I don't want to be associated with an asshole, anyway."

The both of us remain silent during the rest of the wait. So quiet that I can hear him typing away at his phone while I look around at all the yellow coats and purple umbrellas walking from left to right, and vice versa. It sure gets rainy in this town, and it still surprises me how the folks around here can remain so optimistic even as they're being drenched.

Minutes later, the yellow bus pulls up. Ace gets on first, finding a seat in the back, while I drag behind and scoot into a seat near the front, alone. The rest of the kids on the bus look like us, white button-down shirts with blue plaid skirts for the girls, and khaki pants for the boys.

The ride down the road is bumpy, hitting a pothole every time we pass a light or a stop sign. I can hear Ace in the back chatting it up with another boy, laughing and joking around, while I remain silent with my earbuds in, trying to ease the anxiety creeping up on me.

The town of Ojai just seems so strange the more I look at it. More and more yellow coats with purple umbrellas grace the streets, with people still unfazed by the harsh weather that's pouring down on them. And why are they all dressed the same? It's like I'd left a town of normalcy and moved into some sort of cult.

When the driver stops, a bunch more students hop

on. One of them is a boy about my age with dark brown hair and emerald green eyes. I can feel my body tingling when he decides to sit next to me.

"Hey, I'm Daven. Daven Porter," he says to me, extending a hand out.

I pull my own hand out from the pocket of my blazer and shake it. "Bella Nova."

"Bella, I like that name. It's very sweet." He points to my right hand. "Cool ring, by the way."

He flashes a smile at me, one that makes me want to just collapse in his arms. But no, I can't. Not again. Before moving to Ojai, I made a promise to myself and my mother that I would try and restrain myself more when it comes to boys. I can't let myself fall for the first one who says I have a sweet name.

"Thanks," I reply, quickly pulling my hand away.

"So, Bella, are you new? I haven't seen you around town before, and I know everyone. My father's the town mayor, so it's my duty to know all the residents here."

I nod. The mayor's son? Even hotter. "My family just moved here from Oregon yesterday."

"Oregon, interesting. Portland? My parents like to take my sister and I to Mount Hood every winter to ski. We always have so much fun there."

I shake my head. Even though I'd lived in Oregon my entire life, I never really left Astoria. There was just never any reason to.

"Astoria."

"Never heard of it."

"It's a little coastal town in northern Oregon, near the border of Washington. Many people don't know about it."

"Why the move here?"

I'm starting to realize that this isn't just another two-second conversation, that Daven is going to keep talking to me even though I have earbuds in. Slowly, I pull them from my ears, grip them into a ball, and tuck them into the side pocket of my backpack.

"It's a long story," I manage to get out without choking up. "We just wanted a change, that's all."

I'm trying to escape my past, not relive it. No way in Hell am I going to disclose the story of my entire tragic past to some cute boy I just met.

"Let me guess, a memory you'd rather just forget?" He turns and smiles at me, his eyes showing a complete understanding to my situation.

"Something like that." I smile back.

When the bus finally pulls up to the front of the school, Daven escorts me off the bus.

"How would you like a personal tour guide on your first day? I know how daunting it can be arriving on a campus you're not familiar with. Also, it doesn't help that this campus has eight buildings." He chuckles and pulls out his phone to check the time.

"I'd love that."

I turn around and see Ace still chatting it up with the boy from the bus. I'm not sure what he's up to, but I bet it's nothing good.

"Come on!" Daven gestures to me as the bell rings, and I follow him into the main building.

Despite being over a thousand miles away, Villanova Prep looks just like Astoria High, the school separated into their own cliques, from the popular cheerleaders to the burly jocks to the stoners sheltered in the janitor's closet and getting high during study period. Ace and the boy from the bus walk straight into that one.

Immediately, I know there's a slim chance that I'll fit in with any of these crowds. I'll probably just resort to eating lunch alone in a bathroom stall, much like Cady Heron in Mean Girls, when no one at her new school wanted her.

"Hey, Daven!"

"Looking sharp, Daven. Looks like you worked out this summer."

"Sexy as ever, Daven. I'll see you around."

When we walk in, all the girls in the hallway start flirting with him, like he's a piece of meat thrown into a pit full of lions. It's clear that Daven Porter is the Brick Cannon of this school, the Alex Shaw, the Billy Styles. It's no wonder why I found myself instantly attracted to him.

"Now, now, ladies, settle down. There's only so much of me. I can't give my attention to all of you," he says to them.

"Aw, then at least choose one of us!" A blonde girl starts to whine. "It's Junior year. Don't you think it's about time that you stop being single and choose one of us? Preferably me?"

He chuckles and turns to her. "Stephanie, Stephanie, Stephanie. You know better than anyone that I can't do that. If I date one of you, the rest of you will just get angry. What'll happen to your friendship then?" He reaches out a hand and tucks a strand of hair behind Stephanie's ear, making her blush. "Besides, I'm sort of enjoying all this attention. Makes me feel special."

"You *are* special!" Stephanie agrees, blushing again with the rest of the group giddy behind her.

"Anyway, I should really get going." Then he points to me. "This is Bella. She's new, and I want you all to be nice to her. Got it?"

As they all nod, Daven leads me away. I can hear a sigh of relief coming from him. And I don't blame him. If I had that many people fawning over me, I'd feel stressed out, too. But then again, it's a problem I'll never have to worry about. I'm always the one chasing, never the one being chased.

"Is it true?" I ask as we walk down the hall in the opposite direction.

Daven looks at me and smiles. I'll never grow tired of that charming smile. "Is what true?"

"That the only reason you're single is because you don't want them to kill each other."

"Ha! Of course not. It was the only thing I could think of to let her down easy. They're all obsessed with me, or more so, they're all obsessed with my father's money. The girls in this school are all the same. Instead of trying to succeed and make their own money, they'd rather chase after someone with a rich family. It's a bit sickening, actually. And there's definitely no chance that I'd ever go out with one of them, especially not the cheerleaders. They're all ditzes."

"Wow, I never would've guessed how you truly feel based on that conversation back there. At first, I thought you were just—"

"Shallow?" he finishes for me. "I can see why you might think that. But it's all for show. I have a reputation to uphold, after all. If word gets out that the mayor's son is walking around school being an obnoxious dick, he'd lose all his supporters. Plus, I'm student body president. I need to keep up this façade if I have any chance of winning again next year."

"So... would you ever date? Even if it's not one of them?"

He whips his head over and grins at me. "Why? Are you interested?"

And that's when my face turns red as I quickly force myself to shake my head and look away. "Just curious, that's all."

Out of the corner of my eye, I notice that he quickly turns his head away also, rubbing the back of his neck with his hand and letting out a small chuckle. "Yeah... yeah, same. Just curious." He looks down at his watch, probably for some sort of distraction from this conversation. "We should really get going. I don't want you to be late for your first class. It wouldn't be very student body president of me if I let that happen."

His grabs my hand and picks up his steps, my little feet fiddling behind, but I don't mind.

Am I falling for him already? It's only the first day of school, and I'm already getting myself in trouble?

During lunch, I can hear the whispers and laughter directed at me when I walk into the cafeteria. It's beginning to grow clear to me that these people are not welcoming of newcomers, for fear of them disrupting their little cliques. Some things just never change.

After grabbing my lunch, I walk past the cheerleaders, with Stephanie Grimes, the obvious Queen Bee, cackling and hissing insults in my direction. At that moment, I want nothing more than to take my tray and dump it over her fresh perm, watching the milk and yogurt drip down her face and ruining her makeup.

But I can't. I have to remain strong and restrain myself to avoid my parents sending me to yet another school. So, instead, I grit my teeth, grinding them hard against each other to prevent myself from saying something I'd regret.

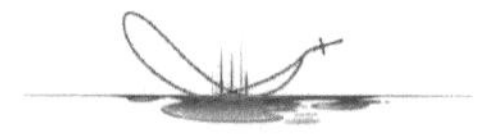

SEVERAL HOURS LATER, I find myself anxiously staring at the clock, waiting for the final bell to ring.

My first day at Villanova Prep isn't anything to brag about or take home. It's not like it's anything I haven't experienced before. The same crap as my old schools. Stuck up girls, and brawly, dumb meatheads. And although Daven has been nice to me, I still ate lunch alone. Ace was nowhere to be seen, not even in the cafeteria. I just hope he shows up for the bus.

"Hey, Bella!" I hear someone shout from behind me.

Thinking it's Ace, I plaster on a stern look on my face before turning around, just to see Daven running toward me. I quickly force my stern face into a smile.

"Hey, Daven."

"How was your first day? I'm sorry I wasn't around much. The student council had meetings all day, and between that and classes, I barely had any time for myself."

"It's fine." I shrug.

I can't tell him the truth, that I had to eat alone, that I had to thwart the evil stares of the cheerleaders and the inappropriate advances of the jocks. I can't have him knowing what a shitty first day I had, and how Daven's probably my only friend. I can't have him thinking I'm a loser.

"You're not mad at me, are you? Because I wasn't there?"

I shake my head. "No, of course not. It's been a long day, that's all."

He let out a sigh. "Whew! That's a relief!"

"Does it bother you if people are mad at you?"

"Nope!" He puts his hands on my shoulders. "It bothers me if *you're* mad at me."

As he says that, a wave of awkward tension washes over us, and silence lingers in the air for a few brief moments.

"Bella! Let's go!" The shrieking sound of Ace's voice breaks the strain between us, and I couldn't be happier.

"I have to go," I finally manage to say.

"I'll see you tomorrow?"

As I nod, I can hear Ace shouting my name again, so loud that I'm sure the rest of the school can hear him, too. But Ace has never been one to care whether the world sees him as a lunatic. He's just Ace, a free-spirited, obnoxious loud mouth.

During the ride home, I pop in my earbuds and slowly let my mind wander away. One day down, just a hundred and seventy-nine left to go. It's going to be a rough year for sure. The rain continues to pour down on the roads outside, the yellow coats and purple umbrellas still passing by each other with almost robotic waves of hello. There's definitely something going on with this town. Or maybe, I'm just not used to all the friendliness.

Suddenly, I feel a slight tap on my shoulder. Expecting it to be Ace, I whip my head around, but am greeted by no one. There isn't even anyone sitting directly behind me, and I start to turn red. After the day I had today, I'm just not in the mood for any pranks, especially not from Ace. There's only so much I can deal with in one day.

When the bus arrives at our stop, I grab my bag and walk off, Ace skipping behind toward me.

"Why so fast? Got someone else you gotta murder?"

I stop, my rage growing even more intense. "What the hell's your problem?"

He backs away. "Whoa, chill the fuck out. It's just a joke!"

"Not that! Why'd you tap me on the bus earlier and just disappear? Is that supposed to be funny?"

"What the hell are you talking about? I was nowhere near you."

"Just lay off, Ace. Just lay off!"

I angrily storm away, in the opposite direction of home. I don't care that it's pouring, and I'm getting drenched. I don't care that Mom will throw a fit because I'm late. I don't care that I'm wandering around a town I barely know all alone. I hate it here!

I can hear my phone ring in my pocket, but I just ignore it. It's probably Ace, calling to make sure I'm not dead so Dad won't kill him for showing up to the house without his sister. Whatever. He deserves whatever he has coming his way.

There's a canal near our home that I hadn't noticed when we first moved here. I was too busy having nightmares about my past in the car to focus on my surroundings. But it's beautiful, even in the midst of a rainstorm. The green lily pads floating on the naturally blue water, such a beautiful and calming sight to see. I can just sit here for hours staring out into its beauty, if the pouring rain wouldn't get me sick.

But still, it doesn't hurt to live out that dream a little. Dropping my bag down on the wet asphalt, I draw my blazer over my head and plop myself onto the concrete. The puddle of water soak through my skirt, but I don't care. With all the craziness in my life, I just need a moment of peace to forget about it all.

What am I doing with my life, anyway? I can't keep forcing my family to move every time I fuck up. I should be in prison right now, not a prep school. My parents had been understanding enough to take me away, but that also makes them accomplices, and I can't have them keep covering up for my falls.

I lean back on my hands, my fingers brushing against gravel and rocks. Gosh, I can't even remember the last time I've felt so connected with nature. Fishing for a fairly large rock, I pick it up and chuck it into the canal, the sound of the quiet plop like music to my ears.

Brick and I went by the bay once, his favorite spot near Youngs Bay that he said he'd like to go to every now and then to relax and clear his mind. It's a large empty field of absolute nothingness, a quiet and isolated part of town that barely gets any traffic. I remember the day he suggested a picnic during a sunny afternoon, beer in hand with a basket full of sandwiches and fruit. Though, it wasn't like we really did any eating. One beer in, and Brick was already all over me, climbing on top of me and tearing my clothes off. Looking back now, I wonder if that was actually a spot he took all his victims. Even the thought of it sends chills up my body.

Then I hear another plop, the sound of another rock splashing into the canal. Is someone else here? I turn my head to look around, curious to see who else is crazy enough to stand here, throwing rocks in the dead of a thunderstorm.

But I can't see anyone. Maybe it's because of the haze from the storm, or they're hiding in the shadows somewhere that I'm not aware of, but to me, I'm all alone. Strange. It better not be Ace. But then again, Ace would never be out here. He spends all his time indoors, either playing video games or getting high. Nature sickens him, his own words.

The rain continues to pour down even harder; time for me to go if I don't want to get sick. I press my hands against the concrete to hoist myself up, grab my backpack, and start heading home.

When I get back, I'm lucky enough to find that Mom and Dad are still at work. Ace is home, his door shut with his usual "Bella not allowed" sign stuck on his bedroom door. I roll my eyes. Whatever. I don't need him.

So, I walk into my own room, closing the door behind me before changing into some dry clothes. Sweatpants and an oversized sweater are usually my go-to. Why sacrifice comfort to look pretty for no one? I then throw myself onto my bed and pull out my phone. A missed call from Daven. So, it was him who called earlier, not Ace. How'd he even get my number?

Nonetheless, I decide to call him back. There's never any harm in seeing what a cute boy wants. For now, anyway.

"Hello?" A deep voice picks up on the other line.

"Hey, Daven. It's me, Bella."

There's a pause on the other end.

"Bella! I'm so glad you called back! I was beginning to get a little worried."

Worried? Was he worried about me? Does he care about me?

"Sorry, I was busy earlier. I must've missed it. How'd you get my number, anyway?"

He chuckles, and I can tell that he's smiling on the other line. "I guess that's a little creepy, isn't it? I forgot to mention. I also work in the school office. I pretty much have access to everyone's records."

"You're not going to come over here and murder me, are you?" I joke.

"Nah, no way! You're too pretty to die. I just feel really bad about not being there for you on your first day, and it felt like our conversation earlier ended on a sour note. I don't want you to hate me, Bella."

"Why do you care so much about what I think of you?"

I can tell where this conversation is heading, and even though I knew I shouldn't, I can't stop myself. Daven is just too charming.

"Because... because I like you, Bella. You're

different from all the other girls, especially those ditzy cheerleaders. You're real, and super, super pretty."

I put down my phone and smile, hands over my mouth to prevent a squeal of excitement from coming out.

"Would you like to go out with me, Bella? Just one date? And if you hate it, I promise to never bother you again."

I nod, but then quickly realize that he can't see it. Clearing my throat to avoid sounding too enthusiastic, I whisper, "Yes, I'd love to go out with you."

"Oh, wow, I'm so excited that you said yes! Honestly, I'd never asked anyone out before. I never found someone who seemed like a right fit until I met you. I was so nervous that you'd say no. How about tomorrow after school? Meet up after our last class for burgers and milkshakes?"

"Sounds like a plan," I whisper again before hanging up.

I can't keep myself from smiling from ear to ear. I have a date with Daven Porter, the cutest guy in school *and* the son of the mayor. It's risky. Daven seems nice enough on the outside, someone reputable enough to not put me in a position where I have to move again. But then again, that's what I thought when I dated all the others.

Just one date. One date can't hurt, and if I start to see any sign of evil, then I'll immediately cut it off. It's a plan I'm sure I can commit to.

CHAPTER 4

"Brick, what is all this? Who are all these women?" I turned around to face him, holding a stack of photos of different women, all either partially undressed or completely naked.

He winked at me. "Nice collection, isn't it? You'll be part of it very soon. Isn't that exciting?"

"What are you talking about? Part of what?"

Suddenly, he pulled a knife out from behind his

back, the blade shiny and the tip sharp. He had an evil look on his face, so evil that I couldn't look away but also couldn't look directly at. And before I knew it, he lunged at me, piercing my wrists with his hands while holding the blade in his mouth.

"What are you doing? Get off! Get the fuck off me!" I screamed and tried to pry myself away from his grip, but he was twice the size of me. It'd be a miracle for me to escape.

"It's what you wanted, right?" he asked, his voice menacing and mocking. "To be with me forever? Well, this is your chance!"

I continued to kick and squirm, whatever I could to escape from his grasp. I could smell the disgusting stench of coffee and cigarette on his breath, and it made me want to vomit.

"No! Stop it, Brick! Let me go!"

My foot eventually found its way to the lower half of his body, and with one swift kick, he came tumbling down, his hands grasped around his balls. I quickly pulled myself up and started running, tripping over myself from the distress and distraught. But I could still hear him coming after me from behind, coming in fast, and I knew I had to bolt.

Another trip later, I found a gun, a small pistol below my feet, and I knew it was my saving grace. I turned around and pointed it at him.

"Stop, Brick! Come any closer, and I'll shoot." My voice was shaking, my confidence hesitant, and he could sense it.

It didn't faze him one bit, and he grunted and charged closer to me. I closed my eyes, afraid for my life, and pulled the trigger. A loud thump was soon heard against the ground, and when I opened my eyes again, there he was, lying face down, blood pouring from his body.

MY ALARM RINGS, and I spring out of bed, gasping for air. It's all just a dream, a horrible, horrible dream. I don't expect these memories to stop appearing any time soon, but just for a night or two, I'd like a break so I can at least get some sleep.

I can see Daven standing in the front yard of the main building when I got off the bus. He walks over to me, greets me with a hug, and pulls a yellow daisy from behind his back.

"For you." He smiles.

"What's this for?"

"Our date later, silly! You didn't expect me to show up empty-handed, did you? I wouldn't be a gentleman if I did."

I smile, my heart beating even faster when he grabs onto my hand and squeezes it tight. "You're a gentleman?"

"Father taught me well. I'm as gentle as any man can be!"

He starts to laugh, and I join in alongside him.

That's when he briefly stops and looks over at me. "You're so cute when you laugh," and leans over to kiss me on the cheek.

I let him continue. I want it all, his touch, his affection, his everything, and he knows it.

When we both enter through the front doors and into the hallway, I can feel all eyes on us, especially the death glares of the girls. Rather than their usual flirtatious greetings to Daven, it's obvious that they want to cut in between us and tear us apart. And no one wants to do that more than Stephanie.

"What in the actual fuck, Daven?" she asks. "I thought you said you're not dating anyone!"

"I'm not," Daven answers her, gripping my hand tighter.

"Oh, really, then what the hell is this?!" Her gaze starts to travel down, stopping at where our hands joined.

"Oh, this? Bella and I aren't dating. Not yet, anyway. Our first one's later this afternoon."

I'm actually surprised by how nonchalantly he said that, like he doesn't care whether he offends anyone. That only turns me on even more.

But I can't say the same for Stephanie.

"Dating?! Her?! Why? She's... she's so... plain," she finally finishes, wrinkles forming on her forehead from the look of disgust that she throws over at me. "Wouldn't you rather go out with someone pretty and popular, like me?" She spins around, her cheerleader outfit flying out and exposing the underwear she's wearing beneath it. All the boys around her can't stop staring, but Daven doesn't seem to pay any attention.

"I'll stick with Bella," he calmly says and looks over at me.

He then leans down and kisses my cheek again, my face turning red.

It made all the other girls fume. I can almost see the smoke coming out from their ears, and for once, I feel less alone. I have Daven. If no one else, the one person who actually matters is here for me.

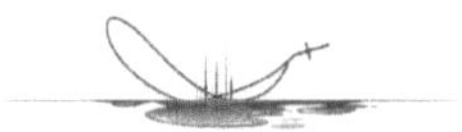

AFTER SCHOOL, Daven and I met up by the flag pole for our date. He gave me another hug, longer this time, and we both walked to the diner that's close to campus. He told me to choose a booth while he went up to order our food: the greasiest cheeseburger for each of us and chocolate shakes.

"I'm so glad you're not vegan," he says with a mouthful of burger. "You have no idea how obsessed everyone in that school is about eating strictly vegan, gluten-free, non-GMO, sugar-free, keto-based foods."

"They eat air?" I ask lightheartedly.

That made him laugh. "Pretty much!"

"Can I ask? What is it about me that made you want to go out with me? I'm not pretty like Stephanie and all the other cheerleaders. They had a point. I'm really just sort of plain."

"I don't think that at all." He scoots out from his side of the booth and joins me, pressing his body next to me and wrapping his arm around my shoulders. "I think you're way prettier and way better than them. You're humble, real, like I can be myself around you without worrying that you're only in it for the money."

"I don't care about money."

"Exactly! And I sensed that when I first met you. You're just so unique and special, Bella."

I turn my head slightly and can see him staring at me, as if he's peering through my eyes and into my soul. "Why are you staring at me like that?"

"Sorry." He blushes. "But I'm just wondering what it would feel like to kiss you right now."

"You can if you want," I reply shyly.

And just like that, he wraps his other arm around me and pulls me in, staring into my eyes a bit more before leaning in with his face. His lips taste sweet, and although he said he'd never dated before, his lips say otherwise as they caress against mine. I find myself melting like butter into his arms, my body falling prey to the power he seems to have over me.

"Wow," he whispers when he pulls away slightly.

And before I have a chance to say anything, he pulls back in and begins caressing my lips again. I've had many kisses in my past, some great, others pretty terrible. But this? This is definitely my best to date.

After we finished the rest of our food, Daven insists

that he walks me to the bus stop before parting ways. "I want to make sure you're safe. I want to protect you."

He kisses me softly on the lips again and grabs my hand to leave. The storm is still pouring when we walk out, and I continue to watch the yellow coats and purple umbrellas cross our path. That's when Daven pulls out his own purple umbrella.

"What's with the purple umbrella?" I ask. "Why does everyone around here dress the same when it rains?"

"You know, I've actually never noticed that. My guess is that yellow coats and purple umbrellas are all we sell around here. People will have to drive all the way to LA if they want a different color, and it's definitely not worth all the trouble."

"That explains a lot. I was starting to think I'm going crazy."

"You're definitely not going crazy."

He pops open his umbrella and pulls me in under it, shielding me from the wet droplets falling from the sky. I feel safe in his arms, like he can never do anything wrong and will never hurt me. When we finally get to the bus stop, he turns to me and asks.

"Bella, I really enjoyed our date. Like, really. And I know it's only our first, and we still have a lot to learn about each other, but would you like to be my girlfriend?"

Boy, he moves fast! And here I am thinking I'm the only one. I made a promise to myself that I wouldn't date at all for the remainder of high school, but Daven is someone that even my strict father would approve of. It's just too hard to turn down.

"I'd love to."

He kisses me again, his arms wrapping around my waist and holding me close until we both hear the bus pull up.

"Call me when you get home?" he whispers.

I nod again and climb onto the bus, waving goodbye to my new boyfriend as the bus drives away.

During dinner later that night, my mother notices the change in my attitude.

"Looks like someone had a good day today. Bella, honey, why are you smiling so much?"

I can't tell her about Daven, not yet, anyway. It'll bring up too many questions, and it'll only make my father throw a fit about having to move again.

"I bet it's a boy," Ace chimes in. "Bella's only ever happy when she has a new boy toy."

I grab a bread roll and throw it at him.

"Ace! Be nice! And Bella, stop throwing your dinner." My father looks up from his plate long enough to lecture us before returning to his steak.

"It's nothing, Mom. I just had a good day at school."

Ace is onto me, and I can't have him exposing me to our parents before I'm ready.

"Well, I'm glad, sweetie. It's good to see that things are turning around for you."

"I still bet it's a boy," Ace mumbles under his breath.

"Ace!" Mom hisses at him, shutting him up during the rest of dinner.

I can hardly fall asleep later that night. I can't stop thinking about my new school life now that I'm Daven Porter's girlfriend. I'll definitely be treated differently, by the cheerleaders especially. But for once, I'll be part of the popular crowd, part of the table at lunch that everyone wants to sit at. For once, I'll actually be someone.

I decide to send one final text to Daven, telling him that I can't wait to see him tomorrow, before climbing into bed and pulling the sheets over my head. Maybe with this new change in mood, I'll finally stop having nightmares about my past.

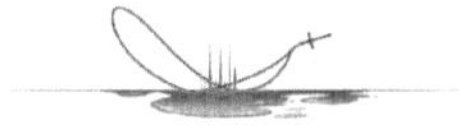

"Bella, Bella Nova," a mysterious and deep voice calls out to me.

"What? Who is it? Who's here?"

I wake up, and while I'm still wearing my pajamas, I'm no longer in my bed. Instead, I find myself lying in some sort of cave, like a hole that has been dug underground and is beginning to heat up like a sauna.

"Hello?" I call out again.

I place a hand on the ground. "Ouch!" The black asphalt feels nothing like the ground by the canal. This feels almost... squishy? Warm and squishy, like there's a pool of lava sitting beneath it.

As I look around, I see a dark and shadowy figure fly by my vision. I can't quite make out what it is, but whatever it is, its skin is dark as night, and I'm pretty sure I saw horns. Maybe a ram? Or a different type of animal?

I've enjoyed a hike or two in my lifetime. Growing up in Oregon, I sort of had to if I wanted to spend time outdoors. But never have I, or will I, ever dreamt of spending the night in a cave with a wild animal. I still have so much to live for, so much to see. And my relationship with Daven, I can't die just when it's starting!

I quietly stand up, brushing the dirt off my sweatpants and straightening out my sweater. What is that? Dare I follow it? Or will it jump out and eat me alive? My mind tells me to stay put until someone comes to save me, but my body is curious to see what the dark figure around the corner is. Without being aware of it, my legs start moving, moving and moving toward the large rock in the corner where the figure seemed to have bolted off to.

But then I hear another whisper, a female voice this time. "Bella, Bella, wake up."

"Mom?"

"Bella, Bella, it's time to wake up," the voice says again, followed by the blaring sound of my alarm.

"I'm up! I'm up!" I spring up on my bed and shout.

Mom looks at me, startled by my sudden reaction. "Bad dream, honey?"

I look around, finding myself back in my own bedroom. It was all just a dream, a strangely realistic dream. "Yeah, something like that."

When I finished getting ready and came downstairs, Ace is already gone. He had taken the bus alone this morning since Daven called last night and said he'll be picking me up. He's one of the few students at Villanova Prep who has his own car, and so it's a privilege to be seen in one.

I turn to the mirror by the stairs and take a look at myself one more time. Today is my first full day as Daven Porter's girlfriend, and I want to look absolutely perfect for him. I quickly ruffle a few fingers through my hair, combing through a few knots, when my phone rings, and it's Daven, telling me he's parked just around the corner. Mom and Dad still don't know about him. I told them I made some friends at school and am getting a ride with one of them. It's not technically a lie. They just happen to think the friend is a girl.

I grab my phone to send a short message back, telling him I'm on my way. Then I fish out my lip gloss from my bag and quickly polish my lips before smacking them to complete the look. Perfect. Well, as perfect as I can be.

"Bye, Mom! I'm heading out!" I call out to my mother in the kitchen.

"Stay safe, dear!" She yells back, followed by a few other words I missed as I shut the front door behind me.

I don't know why I feel so nervous. I mean, Daven

and I have kissed, and we're so comfortable around each other that I feel like we're best friends. But maybe part of me still has suspicions about him, that maybe this is all a game, and when I least expect it, he'll turn on me. No. I shake my head. He won't do that. He won't!

I ruffle my hair a bit more and unbutton a few more buttons of my blouse while heading over to where he's waiting. As I approach, he quickly gets out from his convertible and greets me with a long hug and a passionate kiss on the lips.

"You look stunning. Sexy as sexy can be," he whispers to me and pulls me into him once more.

"So do you," I whisper back.

"Oh, hey! I got something for you." I watch as he skips over to his car and pulls out a gift box. "Open it."

"What is it?" I ask.

"Just open it. You'll love it. Trust me."

Carefully, I undo the bow and open the red lid. Inside is a red and black wrist corsage with gold trimmings along the rim of the petals. "This is the most beautiful thing I've ever seen."

"And it's all for you." He takes the box from me, pulls out the corsage, and carefully places it around my wrist. "Bella Nova, will you do me the honor of going to the homecoming dance with me?"

A homecoming dance. I had never been to one before. It wasn't like my previous schools didn't have one; I was just never invited to one. Nor have I ever been invited to prom. But now, I have another chance.

A chance to finally go to a school dance with, dare I say it? My boyfriend, the hottest guy in school, and he's all mine.

I try to contain my squeal, but as soon as he said those words, it all comes pouring out like a little girl in an ice cream store. But he found it charming, nonetheless, and I couldn't be happier.

When we arrive at school, he rushes over to open the passenger door for me, an act of a true gentleman. I can't wait to walk inside and see the mouth of the cheerleaders all drop at the corsage Daven had given me. Finally, I have something that the popular kids don't, and I love it.

"Hey, Daven." Stephanie approaches us as soon as we walk in. "Got a date to homecoming yet? I just bought the sexiest red strapless dress. Cost me nearly a grand, but it's totally worth it. I'm thinking I can get you a matching red suit to go along with it." She dances her fingers along his shoulder, but he quickly brushes them off.

Good.

"First of all, Stephanie, I'm not an accessory. And second, I already have a date. Bella."

He lifts up my hand and shows her the corsage. All the other girls gasp and rush over to admire the beautiful rose neatly placed on my wrist. Well, all but Stephanie.

"Her?! You're really choosing her, plain Jane, over me? Do you not realize that I'm the prettiest one on this entire campus? Guys literally trip over themselves to go out with me, and you're turning me down? For her?!"

Daven ponders over it for a moment, clearly playing along, and then finally answers, "Yup!" He turns to me. "Come on, Bella, let's go get the tickets. On me."

As we walk away, I can still hear Stephanie shouting behind us. "You're making a terrible mistake, Daven Porter! You'll regret turning me down! You'll regret it all!"

Later that night, I kiss my corsage and place it down gently on my nightstand. Daven assured me that on the actual day of the dance, he'll replace it with a real one. He just wanted to get me one for now to show me how much he wants to be with me. Such a sweet guy. What will I ever do without him?

I yawn. I had stayed up to three in the morning studying for big test tomorrow, and I feel ready to crash and never wake up again. It only took seconds after my head hit the pillow for me to fall fast asleep.

"Bella, Bella Nova," a mysterious and deep voice calls out again.

I slowly open my eyes and find myself back on that squishy asphalt, my elbows burning as I lean them against the ground. "Ouch!"

"Who's out there?" I call out. "Show yourself! I'm tired of playing games."

Again, out of the corner of my eye, I see a dark figure, dark as midnight, an arm this time, and I follow it as it runs behind the same large rock.

"Gotcha!" I shout when I turn the corner and look behind the rock. Empty. No one's there. Damn it! I was so sure the animal had hidden here, and that I'd find it.

But when I turn back around, I see a monster, a tall and dark monstrous creature with midnight black skin and red eyes. Perched on the top of his head are large horns, resembling that of a ram. I want to scream, run away from the creature and pray for my life. But all that came out is a quiet yelp, followed by me slightly backing away.

The strange thing though, is that this monster is sort of... handsome? And I find myself extremely attracted to him, or it, or whatever it is. Is that weird? He looks so much like Daven! Maybe my immense attraction for Daven had manifested as a dream, and this monster is actually him.

"Who are you?" I ask again. "Daven? Is that you?"

The creature remains silent, but starts to walk over to me. I can't stop staring into his deep red eyes, eyes that look so perfect, pulling me in and enchanting me. Then he touches my face, and I can feel that part of it turning stiff before returning back to its natural state just seconds later.

"Daven?" I ask again.

But the creature shakes his head. "My name is

Draven Asmodeus. I am a demon of the Underworld, and I need your help."

I nearly fall back at his words! "Underworld?"

"Hell."

I spring up on my bed, sweat pouring down my forehead and neck. I look around, and I feel so relieved to find myself back in my own bedroom. The night is still dark, and when I look over at my phone, I still have two hours before the sun rises.

It's all just a dream. It's all just a dream. But even so, why did it feel so real? What the hell have I been eating lately? Ugh, I place a hand on my forehead. I really need to lay off those milkshakes at the diner. I never believed Mom when she told me I'm lactose sensitive. Maybe it's about time I do.

I sigh, rub a hand over my face and fingers on my eyes, and walk into the bathroom. There's definitely something going on with me. Never in my life have I had the same fictitious dream twice in a row. Turning on the faucet, I splash some cold water on my face and climb back into bed.

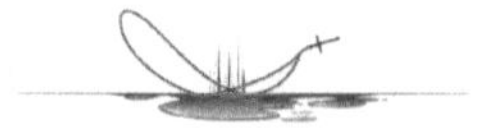

THE NEXT MORNING, I struggle to keep my eyes open when I met up with Daven. He already has a cup of coffee waiting for me, a true lifesaver, but even that isn't enough to keep me awake.

"What's wrong? You look like hell," he says when I walk up to him.

"Thanks..."

"Sorry, I didn't mean it like that. Are you okay? It looks like you haven't slept in days."

He hands me the coffee, and I take a long sip.

"I didn't really sleep well last night. I had a pretty scary nightmare, and it kept me up the rest of the night."

"I've had those before." He reaches over and wraps his arms around me. "And you know what usually helps me get through them?

"A tall glass of warm milk?"

Daven laughs. "That certainly helps! But I was going to say, calling someone. Finding someone to calm me down when I most need it, and ground me back to reality."

"How am I supposed to find someone to call in the dead of night?"

"Easy, me!" He caresses my face. "Bella, you know you can rely on me for anything, right? I love you."

"What?"

He blushes. "I meant to wait and tell you during the homecoming dance, to make it more special, but I've wanted to say it for awhile now. Bella, I love you, ever since I first climbed onto that bus and saw you."

I can't believe my ears. Love? I've never experienced love before. Am I even capable of it?

"You don't have to say anything now," he continues. "But if you ever want to say it back, I'll be here."

"No, I do. I do want to say it because I feel it. I'm just afraid I'll mess it all up and scare you away."

He leans down and plants another passionate kiss on my lips. "Never. Nothing you do will ever scare me away. I love you, with everything I have."

"I love you, too."

That lights a spark in his eyes. "You have no idea how happy I am. What do you say we ditch school for a day and go to the beach, instead?"

"Are you crazy?? It's sixty degrees outside!" I cross my arms over my chest. "Besides, aren't you the one who said you'll never skip school?"

Daven shrugs, and then smiles at me. "I did, and yeah, it is. But there's something I want to show you. What do you say? Do you trust me?"

Mom would kill me if she ever finds out, but I can't help but give into those cute puppy dog eyes of his. "Let's do it."

"Awesome!" He grabs me by the waist and spins me around, planting one more kiss on me before carrying me to his car.

Rincon Beach is a short thirty-minute drive away, a popular spot for tourists, and an even more popular spot for Daven whenever he needs to just get away. I love beaches, but growing up in Oregon, it was always too cold to visit one, even during the summer.

"Here, put this on," Daven turns and says to me after he pulls into the parking lot. He holds up a black blindfold and looks over at me with an expression on his face that says, "Trust me."

Immediately, flashbacks of Brick taking me to the abandoned farm pop into my head. The PTSD is no joke, and I vigorously start shaking my head. I don't even notice that my body is also trembling until Daven drops the blindfold and starts comforting me.

"It's okay, it's okay. I'm sorry, Bella. I didn't mean to offend you or hurt you or anything. I just thought it'd be a good way to surprise you. I'm so sorry. Are you okay?"

I nod, though my body still shaking.

"Tell you what, forget the blindfold. How about you just take my hand and close your eyes?"

"You're not going to kill me, are you?" I ask.

A wave of concern washes over his eyes, and I can tell that he genuinely wasn't trying to hurt me. "I would never, ever, hurt you or betray you. You're my world now, and I only want what's best for you. If you can just trust me with this one thing, I promise you won't regret it."

"Okay," I whisper, taking his hand.

He leads me a few minutes down the beach, my feet sinking in the soft sand with every step, until we finally stop. With my eyes still closed, I can feel the cold breeze of the wind against my skin, and the slight touch of water against my feet as the waves wash up onto the shore.

"Almost there." I can hear him say, the smell of fish and crab reminding me of when I used to sit by the dock back home in Astoria. "Okay," he says again. "Open your eyes."

I slowly open my eyes and am shocked by what I'm seeing. Roses scattered over the sand, forming a large heart, and in the middle, a bottle of champagne and some chocolate-covered strawberries placed on top of a blanket.

"Did... did you do this?" I turn around to ask Daven, who had magically pulled a bouquet of roses from behind his back.

"Ditching school was my plan all along. I was just praying for you to say yes so all this wouldn't go to waste. I drove here this morning before picking you up to set everything up. Do you like it?"

I'm at a loss for words. Daven's treating me like a princess, and part of me still feels like I don't deserve it. I have never been treated like such a queen before, and I still don't know how to act when someone does surprise me.

"I... I love it, but you didn't have to do all this."

"I know, but I wanted to, because you're special." He walks over behind me and wraps his arms around me, snuggling his face into my neck and breathing softly on my chest. "I love you so much, Bella."

Oh, no, not again. I can feel my panties getting wet from his touch, and I can hear my mother in the back of my head telling me to run away if I want to stay out of prison. But it's too late. My body's already melting into his arms as he slowly and softly kisses my neck.

"I want you, Bella," he whispers into my ear and starts to unbutton my blouse.

I let him continue. I don't want to stop him, even

though I know I should. This is Brick Cannon and Alex Shaw all over again, but I don't care. My mind is too far gone, and it's time for my body to speak. He strips me down to expose my bra, letting my blouse fall onto the sand, and caresses my cleavage with his gentle hands before smoothing them up my back and undoing the clasp.

"You're perfect," he whispers again and lays me down on the blanket, encircling my breasts with his tongue before unzipping my skirt and grazing a hand up and down my inner thigh, running his fingers over the bite marks with no questions asked. I feel like I'm in Heaven.

And when he undresses himself and pulls me on top of him, my thighs rubbing against his as our bodies connect into one, I feel like I can finally die happy. He feels so warm inside of me, and the sounds coming from his mouth makes me want him more because I know he wants me.

"I love you, Bella, forever and ever," he heaves as his body continues to jerk in a repetitive motion, and moments later, we both collapse into each other in a state of ecstasy, lying naked on the beach, skin to skin, still connected.

"So, tell me about this dream. What's it about that's gotten you so worked up?" he asks, reaching over for the bottle of champagne and pouring us both a glass.

"Honestly, I don't even know where to start, but I've had the same dream for two days in a row now. And it's some sort of monster with black skin, says he's from Hell, and he needs my help. It's really freaky."

"That *is* freaky," Daven agrees. "Usually, my nightmares are about falling off a tall building or getting run over by a car. I don't think I've ever heard of a dream about a creature from Hell asking for help."

"What do you think it means? Is it bad?"

He shakes his head. "Nah, I think you're just stressed out, or tired. It'll go away soon. I'm sure it's nothing to worry about. Just take deep breaths before you fall asleep." Then he grabs my hand. "But if it comes up again, I'm just one phone call away."

AND SO, that night, I spend ten whole minutes breathing, in and out, in and out, in and out, until I finally breathe myself to sleep. At first, it seems to work, waking up in a French restaurant, wearing a sequin red dress, and being seated at a cloth table in front of Daven, who's dressed in a crisp black suit with a red striped tie.

"Cheers," he says. "To our eight-year anniversary."

"Good evening, sir and madam. My name is Jean Pierre, and I'll be your waiter today. Can I get you started with something to drink?"

"Two glasses of Merlot, please." Daven winks at me. "It's her favorite."

"Coming right up, sir. And would you like to hear about the specials for tonight?"

"Lay 'em on us."

"For the appetizer, we have slow-poached escargots with garlic sauce. The soup for tonight is tomato and fennel, and for the main course, we have the most delicious serving of freshly-caught help me."

I shake my head, taking a minute to register what he had just said. "I'm sorry, what's the main course?" I ask.

"I shall repeat, madam. For the main course, we have the most delicious serving of freshly-caught HELP ME!"

Suddenly, the room starts to shake.

"Daven! What's happening?" I call out.

But instead of the usual comforting voice of Daven reassuring me that everything will be okay, his face begins to melt, revealing nothing but a skeletal structure beneath it. His eyes liquify, and his lips, the lips I had grown fond of kissing, dissolve into a pile of ashes on the tablecloth. The room starts to spin, around and around, all the tables and chairs flying around the room, right before the entire thing gets suctioned into a massive black hole.

And here I am again, finding myself back on that squishy asphalt with the temperature of a whistling kettle. The breathing didn't work. Whatever other crappy advice Daven probably has up his sleeve most likely won't work. It just seems like no matter that I do, I'll always just end up in Hell.

"Welcome back, Bella," the monster named Draven walks out from behind the rock. "I've been expecting you."

"Who are you? And what do you want from me?" I shout, the sound of my voice echoing in the cave.

"You're the chosen one, the one our leader has prophesized would come and finally save us, finally set us free. You are the only one who can help us."

As he speaks, his red eyes glow an even brighter red, as if they're opening up and sucking me in. I force myself to look away, to claw myself toward the opposite direction, but no matter how much I try, the monster is just too powerful.

"I can't help you! I can't! I can't even help myself. Please, whoever you are, leave me alone! Leave me alone! Leave me alone!"

I wake up, covered in sweat. I look over at my phone and sigh that it's only 2am. Another horrible dream. Why does this keep happening? I've never been a fan of horror movies, and I haven't seen one since I was in the fifth grade. I don't understand why I keep having these recurring nightmares.

"I'm just one phone call away." I hear Daven saying in my head. "Night or day, you can always call me."

I reach over for the phone, but then stop. No, I can't. I can't bother him. He needs his sleep. But if I don't, and he finds out that I didn't, he'll be just as angry that I didn't ask for help.

It takes barely two rings before Daven answers.

"Hello? Bella? Is that you?"

"I had another dream," I whisper, trying to avoid waking up my parents.

It's bad enough that I'm up so late on a school night. I can't have them finding out that I'm on the phone with a boy.

Daven's tired voice becomes more alert. "The same dream? Are you okay? What happened?"

"The monster. It just kept saying how I'm destined to save him, how I'm the chosen one. And the red eyes! They're so bright, like they're sucking in my soul. I don't know what to do, Daven. It all just feels so real, and I'm afraid to go back to sleep. What if it's trying to tell me something?"

"I'm sorry, Bella. I wish I'm there in bed with you. So, I can hold you and keep you safe. But my father will kill me if he finds out I'm gone."

"I understand. So will mine."

"But, hey, if you can somehow make it through the night, I promise, tomorrow, we'll go see a psychiatrist. My family knows a great one. Super experienced. He helped my mom get over her post-partum depression after my sister was born. I'm sure he'll have an answer to your dreams. I'm here with you, Bella. I won't let anything happen to you."

"Thanks, Daven. That means a lot. I wish I could kiss you right now."

He starts to make sounds of kissing noises through the phone, which makes me giggle. "When I pick you up tomorrow, I promise to shower you with kisses."

"I look forward to them. Night, Daven."

"Goodnight, Bella. I love you."

I hang up the phone and lie back down against my pillow. I just have to get through the next four hours without falling asleep, and tomorrow, I'll get answers. Just four hours. I can do it, right? I manage to talk myself into calming down a bit, doing whatever I need to just get through the night. And just when I finally start to doze off again, I hear a voice.

"Hello, Bella."

"Whoa!" I nearly leap out of bed at the sound of the voice, grabbing my phone and turning on the flashlight.

At first, there's nothing there. Nothing but the same old bedroom I had grown accustomed to. I slowly shift my light from one side of the room to the other. Nothing. Nothing. And then out of nowhere, I see dark skin, large horns, the creature! He's in my room! But how?!

I want to scream, but I quickly throw my hands over my mouth instead. I thought it was only a dream. What the hell is this?! I start sweating bullets as the creature comes closer to me, and I nearly shit myself when he sits down on my bed.

"Please leave me alone," I whisper quietly, pulling my blanket over half my face.

I close my eyes, squeezing them tight and hoping that it's all part of my wild imagination. Maybe if I count to ten, he'll go away. No twenty. That would be better.

Twenty seconds later, I open my eyes, and he's gone. My room is completely empty again, with no traces of anyone breaking and entering. I let out a sigh of relief. It's just my imagination. It's just my imagination. But all of a sudden, a dark hand grabs onto my left wrist, pulling me down, before I finally kick it and pull away, and the room falls quiet again.

THE NEXT MORNING, my eyes hurt from staying up all night. Part of me still isn't sure whether the whole thing was a dream or just a hallucination. It can't be real. There's no such thing as monsters. Maybe it's finally time to lay off the sugar. A chocolate bar everyday can't be good for me.

I throw the sheets off my body, grab a towel, and walk into the bathroom to shower. When I pull the sweater off over my head, I notice a mark on my left wrist. Not just any mark, but the mark of a large monstrous hand.

"No," I whisper, dropping my towel onto the tiled floor. "No, what? No!"

Throwing my sweater back on, I hug my body close. What's happening to me? Why do I keep seeing things that aren't there?

I jump when my phone starts to ring. It's Daven.

"Hello?"

"Hey, babe, are you doing better? You seemed pretty worked up last night."

"Not really. I think I really do need to go see that psychiatrist. I feel like I'm seeing things."

"Well, you're in luck! I was able to book you an appointment for today. I'll take you over after school. And don't worry, I'll be there with you the entire time."

"Thanks, Daven. You're the best." I smile, briefly taking my mind away from the mark on my wrist.

Daven truly is the best. He's no Brick Cannon. He's no Alex Shaw. He's no Billy Styles. He's simply perfect.

"I love you, Bella."

"I love you, too."

As I hang up, I see something move behind me.

"Mom? Ace? Is someone there?" I call out.

But there's no answer. Mom and Dad should've gone to work by now, and Ace never comes to my room unless it's absolutely necessary.

"Who's there?" I call out again.

Still no answer. I must be losing it.

I walk over to my bathroom sink. Maybe a splash of cold water will clear things up for me. The feeling of the cold against my skin feels so refreshing, so calming. Maybe this is what I needed all along. I then reach over to grab a towel to wipe my face dry, rubbing the soft cotton into my forehead and below my eyes.

"What the fuck is that?" I suddenly yell when I look at my reflection in the mirror.

Close behind me, I see him, the monster, the creature from Hell. His skin black as ash, and his massive horns perched on top of his six-foot body.

Quickly, I throw the towel back over my face and rub as hard as I can.

"It's not real. It's not real." I keep repeating to myself, and when I look back at the mirror, he's gone.

CHAPTER 5

W hen I turn the corner of my street, Daven's standing there, as always, with a cup of coffee and a breakfast bagel in his hands. He greets me with a kiss on the cheek and a light, gentle hug.

"You look like you've just seen a monster," he jokes.

"That's not funny. You don't know what it's been like," I jab back.

"You're right, I'm sorry. That was insensitive." He hands me the paper bag. "I got you your favorite. Bacon, egg, and cheese on an everything bagel. Call this my peace offering?"

My heart melts. He remembered. "Done."

"Dr. Schultz is a legend when it comes to deciphering dreams. I'm sure he can figure out what's going on with you in no time!"

"Let's hope so. I don't know how much longer I can go without sleep."

I finish off the rest of my bagel and climb into Daven's car. The feeling of the breezy wind against my hair feels relaxing, like soft nails are massaging my head. It brings back such wonderful memories of when Mom used to brush my hair and braid it when I was a little girl, a feeling I never want to end.

I turn my head to the side to get more comfortable, catching my reflection in the side mirror... along with the reflection of the creature.

"Shit!" I jump, nearly knocking an arm into Daven, who almost loses control of the wheel.

We begin swerving down the road, Daven trying hard to steady the convertible as I continue shaking beside him. When he finally manages to pull over onto the nearest sidewalk, my heart is still pounding heavily from the initial shock.

"Jesus, Bella! What was that?" he exclaims.

I can tell that he's frustrated, angry even, and I don't blame him.

"I saw it! Him! The monster! He's in the mirror!"

"Where?"

I point over to the sideview mirror where the creature had appeared, but when Daven walks around to take a look, all we can see are our own reflections.

"I don't see anything, babe. Are you sure he was here?"

"I swear! I saw him! The dark skin. The large horns. There's no way I could've mistaken that!"

Daven sighs. "Whatever it was, it's gone now. Let me know if he comes back, though. That meeting with Dr. Schultz can't come soon enough."

I watch, feeling stupid, as Daven walks back around to the driver's side. Am I just hallucinating? It has to be the lack of sleep. I'm just seeing things! It has to be!

Daven continues down the road, and I try to rest my head again, feeling the soft nails massage against my scalp. It's so peculiar how wind can do that. A little too peculiar. I glance over at the side mirror again, and find long black nails attached to long black fingers massaging through my hair and caressing the top of my head. I quickly jerk away, blink several times, but the creature is still there, sitting behind me, staring at me, and grinning.

He's not going away. Why isn't he going away? I blink several more times. I look over at Daven, who has finally regained control of the car. I can't bother him with this again. He'll crash, and it'll be all my fault. I can't have the death of yet another person on my hands. Instead, I fish out my sunglasses from my backpack and pop them on. If I don't see the creature, then he doesn't exist.

"I HAVE a few council meetings today to prepare for the dance on Friday, so I won't be around much. But I'll meet you here after school, okay? So, we can head over together," Daven says to me when we pull up to the school parking lot.

"Sure."

I would rather have Daven by my side at all times. Who knows when this creature will pop up again? But he'd been so sweet and caring thus far, and I'd rather not be an impediment on him.

He gives me a light kiss on the cheek and skips off into a separate building.

When I walk into the main building, Stephanie and her crew are already there by their lockers, polishing off each other's lipstick and comparing the levels of fat on their thighs.

"Well, well, look who we have here! Plain Jane without her shiny knight? What's wrong, Plain Jane? Daven dump you already?" Stephanie begins to taunt.

"Leave me alone," I reply quietly.

"You know, I bet Daven didn't tell you this, but we hooked up yesterday," she continues.

That's when I stop. "What?"

"Ah, so he definitely didn't tell you. It's true, and my girls here can back me up." She points to the crew behind her, who all nod in a robotic motion. "He came over to my house last night, snuck in, and we fucked on my bed." She holds up two fingers. "Twice."

"You're lying. Daven would never do that. He doesn't even like you."

Stephanie laughs. "Well, that's not what he told me last night. The best he ever had, he told me."

My rage begins to build, fists clenching. My entire body is telling me to punch her in her perfect little face and break her perfect little nose.

But suddenly, he appears again, his reflection shining in the mirror behind Stephanie, stroking my hair. I jump and back up against the lockers.

"Stay away from me! Stay away from me!" I start crying.

Of course, this only provokes Stephanie and her little army of blondes to laugh at me even more.

"Wow, Daven really did choose the wrong person. Look at her! She's crazy!"

Sweating bullets, I push past her and bolt down the hallway, running as fast as I can from a creature that I can't even see anymore. I keep going until I reach the girl's restroom. I kick open a stall and drop down to my knees, crying into my hands and praying that it all ends.

And then I hear a knock. I freeze, unsure of who it is or whether they'd heard me. I pull off a wad of toilet paper and hold it against my nose, breathing into it to avoid making any loud sounds.

I hear the knock again, more aggressive this time. What if it's the creature? What if he's come to take me? I hold my breath, shrinking into a ball in an attempt to hide myself.

Then I hear a voice. "Bella?"

Daven! It's Daven. I jump to my feet and unlock the stall.

"Bella, it's me, Daven. Can you please open up?"

I rush over to the main door and unlock it.

"Daven!" I throw my arms around him, holding him close to me, though my body is still shaking.

"Bella, what happened? One minute, I'm in the main office, and the next, I see you running down the hallway. Are you okay?"

My tears continue to drip onto his hands as he caresses my face, forehead to forehead, and he pulls me even closer to him.

"I keep... I keep seeing him. The monster! He won't leave me alone. Make him go away, Daven! Make him go away!"

"Shh, it's okay, Bella. Just breathe. I'm here now. You're safe."

Daven excused himself from the rest of his classes so he could stay with me the rest of the day in the nurse's office. He thought it's some kind of fever, the rise in temperature making me hallucinate things that aren't there, but when Nurse Mary checked me out, I was completely fine. Healthy as the average person.

"You doing okay, Bella? We only have an hour left, and then we can head over to Dr. Schultz." Daven turns to me and grabs my hands with his. "Everything will be okay."

I nod. "Thanks for staying with me. I don't know how I could've made it through the day without you."

"Of course, babe. I love you. I'll always be here for you."

Then I remember what Stephanie had said. "Daven, can I ask you something?"

"Anything you want."

"Did... did you have sex with Stephanie?"

A look of horror washes over his face. "What? Of course not! I'd never do that, even if I weren't with you. Where did you hear that?"

"She told me this morning. Said you went over to her house last night, and that you said she's the best you ever had."

"Bella, Bella, Bella. Stephanie is a liar. A Class A liar. I was home all night with my parents, worried sick about you. I barely even fell asleep because I was expecting a call from you. Don't believe a word she says. Besides, *you're* the best I've ever had. Actually, you're the only girl I've ever been with." He blushes.

"Really? I'm your first?"

He nods. "That's embarrassing, isn't it? But my family is incredibly religious, and I've just been saving myself for the right person. You."

I shake my head. "No, it's not embarrassing. Now, I

feel ashamed for not trusting you, and for not being a virgin."

"It's alright, babe. I understand. The important thing is that we leave the past in the past and just move forward. And you can always ask me anything. I won't be offended."

"I love you, Daven." I lean in and kiss him, his lips so warm that I never want to let go.

LESS THAN TWO HOURS LATER, I find myself sitting on a beige couch in Dr. Schultz's office. Daven, of course, is right there next to me, his arm wrapped around my waist as if he never wants to let me go. I glance around the room. Everything looks good so far. A certificate awarded to Barry Schultz from UCLA, dozens upon dozens of books on his bookcase on multiple personalities and schizophrenic disorders, and best of all, no monsters to be seen.

"Hanging in there?" Daven asks.

I smile at him, right when the door opens, and an elderly man in his sixties, wearing a bolo tie and carrying a large textbook, walks in.

"Ms. Nova, I presume?" I nod as he looks at me before sitting down. "And Mr. Porter, how nice to see you again."

"Dr. Schultz, thank you so much again for agreeing

to see us. How's your son doing? Parker, is it?" Daven asks.

"Oh, that kid is so unmotivated that sometimes I wonder if he's got a loose screw in there. It'll be a miracle if he manages to make it through middle school."

"Give it time. Some kids just develop faster than others. I'm sure little Parker will start shaping up soon enough."

"Let's just hope so." Dr. Schultz then turns to me. "So, enough time wasted. Bella, what brings you in today? Daven here says you've been dealing with some bad nightmares."

"Worse than just nightmares. I think they're haunting me."

He leans back in his chair and rubs his pointer finger and thumb against his beard. "Haunting you? Interesting. I haven't heard that one before. Tell me more about that."

I look over at Daven, who mouths, "It's okay."

"There's this creature, a monster of some sort, in my dreams. He has black skin like tar, large horns, and he keeps saying he's from Hell. At first, I thought it was just a dream. Things usually got better once I wake up. But lately, I start seeing him in my reflection wherever I go. In the mirror of Daven's car, in the mirror at school. It's like this monster is following me, even when I'm not asleep."

"What do you think it is, doc?" Daven asks.

"Hmm, it *is* very peculiar, and Bella here is definitely

experiencing some sort of hallucination. Bella, have you ever been diagnosed with schizophrenia? It's usually brought on by childhood trauma or excessive drug use."

"I've never used drugs, and I don't—" I stop. Trauma, he had said. What if my PTSD is what's causing all of this?

"Bella, you okay?" Daven must've noticed me drifting off into space.

"It seems that Bella here suddenly remembers something. A past childhood trauma, perhaps?" Dr. Schultz starts to say.

I begin heaving. All those memories I'd tried so hard to suppress come rushing back. The gunshot. The blood. Brick.

"Doc, I think we're going to have to come back another time. Thanks for all your help," Daven informs Dr. Schultz before leading me out the door. He grips tightly onto my hand and slowly walks me out. "Oh, yeah, feel free to bill the card on file."

"Will do. Come back anytime, Bella. My door is always open."

I continue to heave, even as we walk out of Schultz's office. "He can't help me," I cry out to Daven. "No one can help me!"

"Don't say that, Bella. This was only your first session. No one's first session goes well. We'll try again another day. But right now, I think we need to get you home so you can rest."

The entire drive back to my place, the both of us

remain silent. I didn't feel like talking, and Daven could sense it, giving me my space. I feel so mentally drained, like the monster had somehow sucked out all the energy inside me.

"Daven," I turn my head over to face him. "Am I a burden to you?" I ask.

"Are you kidding me? Of course not! You can never be a burden. I'm here for you, remember? You need help, and I want to be there for you. Don't ever think that you're impeding me."

"But wouldn't you rather be with someone with less problems? Maybe someone like Stephanie?"

He pulls to a park around the corner of my house, where he usually stops, and turns to me. "Bella, I know whatever Stephanie said to you probably got to your head, but you need to stop self-doubting. I'm with you. You! If I didn't want to be, I wouldn't be here right now, okay? But the important thing now is that you get some sleep."

"But I can't. What if I see... the thing again?"

Daven pauses for a moment. He looks so cute whenever he's serious. "How about you spend the night at my place? My folks won't mind. Just tell your parents that you're staying at a friend's."

He has a point. Ever since I met Daven, Mom has been under the impression that I'd made several female friends at school. She never questions it. And with her attention focused on Ace and his failing grades lately, I don't think she'll mind.

"Sure," I answer. "I'll call my parents on the way. I'm sure they won't mind."

He plants a kiss on my cheek and pulls out of park.

The Porters only live twenty minutes away from my house, and when Daven pulls up into the driveway, my jaw nearly drops. The house is massive! Like a mansion on steroids! But I guess being the mayor of an entire town, Cliff Porter can't risk ruining his reputation by living in a shitty town home.

Daven hops out of the car and shuffles around to open the passenger door for me. He then helps me get up and wraps an arm around my waist, probably to keep me from falling over with how unstable I've been.

As Daven leads me into the mansion, he waves to the gardener, who's manning the most beautiful bed of flowers I've ever seen. And when the maid opens the front double doors, I'm greeted with a magnificent sparkling chandelier, a double spiral staircase, and a hardwood floor shiny enough to eat off of.

"Your house is amazing," I whisper to Daven, who tucks me closer under his arm.

"It *is* pretty extravagant, isn't it? My parents like to go all out when showcasing their status and wealth. Me, personally, I like to keep things minimal. Less is more, I always say."

"Daven! Is that you?" A female voice yells out, and a petite blonde woman, probably only about fifteen years older than me, appears in front of us.

"Mother." Daven reaches over and gives her a hug.

"I want you to meet my girlfriend, Bella. She's staying over tonight. I hope that's okay."

His mother. Jackie Porter. She's so beautiful. Like all the cheerleaders in school merged into one person. I'd seen her on the news before, alongside Cliff, but given her age, I had always assumed that she's Cliff's secretary, not his wife.

"Of course, dear!" She turns to me. "Bella Nova, it's so good to finally meet you! Daven's told me so much about you. Oh, you're such a cute girl. No wonder my son snatched you right up."

"Mom, you're embarrassing me!"

"Oh, Daven, he gets embarrassed by his parents way too easily."

"It's alright, Mrs. Porter. It's really nice to meet you."

"And so polite!" She places a hand on her chest, over where her heart is. "Dinner will be ready in about two hours. Bella, which do you prefer, salmon or tilapia? It's seafood night!"

The choice in dinner is such a new concept to me. Back home, it's always, "eat what's on the table, or don't eat at all." And leftovers are usually the only choice.

"Salmon sounds good," I answer.

"Good choice! That's my little Daven's favorite, too. Now, go enjoy yourselves until then. But oh! Not too much!"

"Mom!" Daven hisses.

He grabs my hand and leads me up the stairs toward his room.

"Sorry about my mother. She can be a little... optimistic."

"It's fine. I don't mind. My mom's usually the same around guests. I like her. She's nice."

"Daven!" A little girl, no more than ten, rushes down the stairs to us. "You'll never guess what happened at school today. Some smelly boy stuck gum in my hair. Gum! And it took mother a hundred hours to get it off!"

Daven laughs and turns to me. "Bella, meet my little sister, CeCe."

"Hi, CeCe, it's nice to meet you."

Daven leans down to the still pouty girl. "And CeCe, you know that when a boy messes with you, it means he likes you, right?"

"Ew, no! I don't like boys! They stink!"

Daven chuckles.

CeCe turns to me. "Hi, Bella. Are you Daven's girlfriend? He talks about you all the time and how pretty you are. You're really pretty."

Now, it's my turn to smile. His entire family is so charming. Now, I see where he gets it from. "I am, and thank you. You're really pretty, too."

CeCe blushes.

"Mom's making fish for dinner tonight. You better go tell her what you want before she gets started."

"Fish?! I HATE fish!" CeCe exclaims and bolts down the stairs.

"She's a bit of a drama queen; don't mind her."

Daven wraps his arm back around me, and we continue up the stairs.

"She's cute."

Then he leans over and kisses me. "Not as cute as you."

Walking into his bedroom, I struggle to believe that his room is part of the house. Everything else inside the house is so extravagant and shiny. But in Daven's room, his gray walls and navy-blue sheets aren't much to look at. And in the center, sitting on his desk, sits a picture frame of the two of us when we went to Rincon Beach. We look so happy together, truly in love.

I pick it up and run a thumb over our faces. "Wow, you weren't kidding when you said you like to keep things minimalistic."

He comes up behind me and wraps his arms around my body, kissing my neck and making me swoon. "Ha, yeah, and that picture right there is my most prized possession."

I spin around, and my lips meet his. He pulls me in by the waist, and we lock lips, tasting each other like we were both starving. He takes off my blazer, dropping it to the floor, before returning his hands back up and unbuttoning my blouse.

"Won't your mom hear us?" I briefly stop him.

"Nah, she always cooks with the music blasting. She won't hear a thing," he assures me and gently leans me down against his bed.

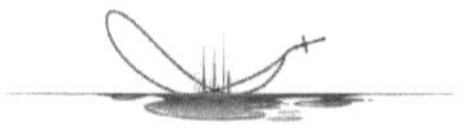

LATER THAT NIGHT, when the rest of the house is asleep, Daven sleeping soundly next to me with his arm still around my bare body, I look around. Even in the comfort of my boyfriend's arms, I'm struggling to fall asleep, terrified of the monster in my nightmare returning.

"Hey, Daven," I softly whisper, waking him up.

"Huh? Bella, what is it?"

"I can't fall asleep. What if the creature comes back?"

"If he does, I'll beat the crap out of him."

"Can you stay up with me for a little longer? Please?"

He sits up a little. "Alright, anything for my girl. Any thoughts on how to keep us occupied?"

"I think I have an idea."

I lean over to him, grabs his face, and paints his neck and chest with my lips. I can hear him slightly moan at the pleasure, right before he grabs my body and flips me over.

Minutes later, Daven is fast asleep, and I find myself alone once again. I begin to doze off, my vision going in and out, until I eventually fall fast asleep alongside him.

"Bella, Bella Nova." I hear a deep, dark voice call out.

I keep my eyes closed. I can already tell who it is. The squishy texture below me certainly doesn't tell me otherwise.

"Why? Why do you keep bothering me? Why do you keep coming into my dreams? What do you want from me? Just leave me alone!"

The creature comes out from behind the rock. But this time, he looks innocent, scared even, like I'm the monster, not him.

"Bella, please, listen to me. I need your help. My family needs your help."

"I can't help you. I can't! Find someone else, please!"

"Bella! Wake up! Wake up!"

I find myself being shaken awake. My eyes open, happy to see Daven's naked bedroom.

I throw my arms around him, shaking. "I saw him again. He keeps saying he needs me to save him. Him and his family. I can't save him. I can't save anyone!"

I break down in Daven's arms, crying my eyes out as he comforts me the rest of the night.

CHAPTER 6

Friday's finally here, and it took Daven days of convincing for me to agree to attend home-coming. Mom even took me shopping to buy me a brand-new dress, a long black sequin halter dress with the back bare, sexy yet elegant at the same time.

Dr. Schultz had given me a small bottle of sleep medication. Well, he'd given it to Daven. I was too busy avoiding monsters to get it. It won't solve my problem, but it's enough to get me through a few nights without completely collapsing.

And the monster. I started seeing him less and less, probably because of the medication. Either that, or he'd gone back to Hell and decided to leave me alone. As long as I stop seeing him, I couldn't care less which option it was.

As I'm getting ready, my phone rings. It's a call from Daven. "I can't wait to pick you up, beautiful."

That's another thing. My parents finally found out about Daven, not that we're dating. No, of course not. But that he's my date for the dance. When they first saw him, they were both shocked that I'm going out with the mayor's son. My father, being the political person that he is, turned their interview into a debate about whether the laws in this town accommodate all races and ages. It was humiliating! But Daven handled it well. He handles everything well. It's why I love him. He keeps me grounded when I'm floating through the air of my own hot head.

"Me, too," then I hang up and walk over to the mirror to put on my makeup. I usually like to keep it pretty natural. A bit of gloss on my lips and some eyeliner. Nothing too fancy. My mother always said I have a natural beauty, and Daven seems to like me just as I am.

As I sit in front of my vanity, lining my lips with the strawberry pink gloss and dousing my wrist with concealer to cover up the monstrous hand print that still resides there, I see a shadow in the corner, coming from my closet. Then I shake my head. I'm just being paranoid. It's probably just a shirt or something.

I look away, but when I quickly glance back at it, the shadow almost looks humanlike, with... with horns? I whip my head around and grab the purple umbrella sitting beside me. Holding the handle up, I slowly make my way over to the closet door. On the count of three, I lift up my foot and kick the door open, only to see my jacket fall off its hanger. A wave of relief washes over me. It's just my clothes. Nothing to worry about. I'm definitely just being paranoid.

I hear the doorbell ring, followed by the sound of my mom's voice. "Bella! Daven's here!"

"Coming!" I call back.

I walk over to my vanity once more and open the drawer to grab a pair of matching earrings, the black pearl ones, to be exact. But beside them, I see my sapphire necklace, the same one that Brick had given me a week before I killed him.

It was my birthday, and we picked up a box of pepperoni pizza to eat together at a park, when he took out the smallest gift box, and inside, was the sapphire necklace. I thought it was the most beautiful piece of jewelry I had ever laid my eyes on, though I haven't seen much during my lifetime. And although every time I see this necklace, I get only bad memories, I still can't find it in myself to throw it away. It has too much sentimental value; I'd rather just hide it behind the rest of my valuables.

Walking down the stairs, I can already hear Dad

chatting it up with Daven about his father the mayor. My dad is a hardcore liberal in a very conservative town, and he usually has much to tell people, even if they don't want to hear it. I can tell that Daven's getting uncomfortable, but he's too polite to ask my father to stop.

"Dad!" I interrupt them. "Daven and I should really get going. We don't want to be late."

Daven's mouth drops open when he stands up and sees me standing by the door. He immediately walks over, ready to give me a kiss, but settles for a long hug instead when I remind him that my parents still don't know we're dating.

"You look so gorgeous," he whispers, pinning the real corsage on my dress.

I mouth a "thanks" and wrap an arm around his waist while my mother snaps a few pictures. Five in, and I realize I have to stop her. If no one does, she usually goes overboard.

"That's enough, Mom. We should really get going."

"Aww, my baby is finally going to her first dance! This is such an exciting moment!" Then she looks at Daven. "Take care of her. Bring her back by nine."

"Yes, ma'am." Daven salutes.

As I follow him to his car, I can't stop staring at how good he looks. The freshly pressed suit really fits him well, accentuating his tone body and muscular arms.

"Your parents seem nice," he says, waiting for me to catch up to him. "Where's Ace? He going to the dance to?"

I shake my head. "Dances aren't really his thing. I'm pretty sure he's hanging out in someone's basement getting high right now."

"Stoner kid, got it. I'm glad you're not into that type of thing."

"And what if I were?"

He smirks. "I guess I'll have to dump your ass."

"Oh, stop it." I hit him lightly with my purse.

"By the way," he leans in and whispers. "You have no idea how much I want to rip that dress off your body. You look so sexy in it."

He pulls the car around the corner after we get in, away from my parents' sight, and kisses me hard on the lips, his gentle hands running up and down my bare back.

"What do you say we just skip the dance and go back to my place?"

"I'd love to, but don't you have to be there? Make sure nothing goes wrong?"

He stops kissing me, and his face drops. "Damn, you're right. After then? I rip that dress off you?"

"Anything you want."

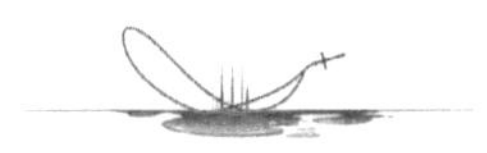

HUNDREDS OF STUDENTS are already standing in the gymnasium when we arrive. Some on the dance floor, while others linger awkwardly by the punch bowl. Gold and black decorations line the room, and bright disco lights sway back and forth. I see Stephanie and her group of cheerleaders at first glance. It wasn't hard, especially when they marched up to Daven and started flirting with him as soon as we walked in.

"Hey, Daven," Stephanie sings. "Like my dress? As you can see, the neckline perfectly lines my cleavage." She winks at him.

"It's alright." Then he turns to me. "I have to run backstage and check on the band. Are you okay without me for a bit?"

"Yeah, but hurry up! I want to dance with you."

"I'll be as quick as a bunny." He kisses me on the cheek and runs off, leaving me with none other than Stephanie.

She let out a breath of air. "You know, Bella, is it? I want to apologize for my behavior toward you. Honestly, I was a little jealous that Daven chose you over me, but I'm starting to come to my senses. And you're not that bad. I'd like to start over. Truce?" she asks, reaching out her hand.

"Are you serious?"

I'm skeptical. Of course, I am! Stephanie and the rest of her crew has done nothing but harass and humiliate me ever since my first day at Villanova Prep. It's hard believing that she'd want to stop now. But then I think about Daven and what he would do. Daven has the soul of an angel, and if he were in my shoes, he'd forgive her. Be the bigger person. It's what Daven would want me to do.

"If I weren't serious, I wouldn't be extending my hand to you. I don't need to touch other people's germs for nothing."

I roll my eyes. "Fine, truce." And I reach out my own hand to shake hers.

"Perfect!" she exclaims. "Because I actually have a little gift for you. It's my way of saying sorry, and that I hope you, and Daven, will forgive me. In fact, I hope that we can become friends. You know, sit together during lunch, go shopping after school, girl stuff. Wouldn't that be fun?"

I wince. Girl stuff? It's never been something I've gotten into. I'd much rather hop on my laptop and binge away my favorite television series. But after everything that happened with Chelsea, I can use a new set of friends, friends I don't end up screwing over.

"I guess." I force a soft smile.

I follow them to where they had placed a large beautifully wrapped pink gift box. I wonder what it is, what could possibly fit inside something like that. Part of me wants to turn the other way. I still don't trust Stephanie. But the other part knows I should, that the reason I'm such a loner is because I don't trust people. And so, I walk over, untie the bow, and open the box.

And out sprays a foul concoction of rotten milk,

mustard, and a brown liquid that I hope to God isn't dog shit.

I scream as the mixture covers my brand-new dress and squirts all over my face, the stench of the blend enough to make me vomit. Why did I trust her? I should've known better than to believe in someone who's been out to get me since day one.

Without even waiting for Daven, I turn around and rush out the door. I can hear Daven calling out after me, but I refuse to stop. Right now, I don't want anything to do with anyone, not even Daven.

I didn't stop until I ran all the way home. Mom and Dad had gone out to dinner, and I open the door to an empty home. Quickly, I rush up the stairs and into my shower, turning on the water and allowing it to drench my entire body, clothes included. Tears pour nonstop from my eyes. My heart feels so broken and betrayed, and I shrink down into the corner of my bathtub, hugging myself and praying that my life ends.

My phone starts to ring when I walk out of the bathroom. Daven. Seven missed calls and counting. But I just ignore him. After the humiliation I went through, I can't trust anyone. Not even him. For all I know, he could've been behind it the whole time. He could've been playing me and on Stephanie's side. They're all against me. Even him.

I walk into my closet and throw on an old sweat-shirt before climbing into bed. My phone rings again. Daven. I turn it off. It's something I'll deal with whenever I feel like it. I reach over to my lamp and switch off the light. Nice and cozy, dark and quiet. Just the way I like it. And just when I begin to doze off, I hear a voice.

"Bella Nova, save me."

FINDING HIM

VIOLA TEMPEST

UNLEASHING HELL BOOK TWO

LOVING HER

VIOLA TEMPEST

CHAPTER 1

It's time. We've waited for five thousand years for this very moment. Five thousand years trapped inside this treacherous body, haunting me for millennia. But now, now is the time for our redemption, to take back what rightfully belongs to me and my family. The ground rattles and shakes, a sight I've longed for, for more years than I dare to count.

It's time for the humans to suffer like we have. I walk closer to the surface of the Earth, listening to their mundane conversations above me, and I chuckle. That light vibration, barely a quiver in the grand scheme of things, and they're already whimpering like the dogs they are. All that money, all that pride and pretense, I'm surprised the little earthquake hasn't sent them running for their rockets to jet off toward the stars in fear.

I don't hate humans, not entirely. They're an ignorant breed, but I can't hate them when I was once *one* of them, walking through life as oblivious to the universe as they are. If I hadn't fallen to the tragedy of living in the Underworld, I would never have come to the realization that it's important not to make enemies of others.

I've spent centuries regretting my actions. Why had I been so rash? Why didn't I just keep my opinions to myself? If I had, none of us would be in this mess. I ruined my life, and the lives of my family; they're paying the price for my mistakes. I was young, I was impetuous, but they were persecuting *us* because we were different. Didn't that mean *anything* to them?

Of course, I was going to defend my people; of course, I was going to scream bloody murder. Should I have known better? Yeah, of course, I should have. I didn't help my family in the slightest; I only made things a hundred times worse than they already were.

I proved those ignorant human fools right; I proved their point... but could they have maybe had a little compassion for us as well? Was that too much to ask?

"Charlie! Grab the keys! Grabs the beans and the

chicken! It's happening! The apocalypse is nigh!" I hear an elderly woman shout above my head.

"Goodness, Betsy, how many goddamn times have I told you? It's not an apocalypse; it's just a little earthquake!" The elderly man, Charlie, replies.

"Whatever it is, I'm not about to stand up here and risk it. We need to get to the bomb shelter. Did you go to the Nova's? Are they coming?"

"I tried knocking on their door, but no one answered. Come on, before it gets any worse."

"I thought you said it was just a 'little' earthquake?!" Betsy snaps back, their voices growing dim as they move away from where I stand.

I chuckle. Just a little earthquake. I can understand why they might think that. I mean, who *really* expects the beginning of the end? Their innocence is amusing to me. Betsy's right, though. She's one of the few lunatics who actually aren't as crazy as the world thinks they are.

If only they really knew what happened every thousand years; if only they remembered or even believed the stories their ancestors left behind for them. If only they knew; if only they *believed* that every thousand years, the ground reopens, and the creatures of the Underworld travel to the surface to reclaim what had once been theirs. The ultimate battle between two species, where neither side is guaranteed safety. Maybe if they knew, they would be more forgiving... or at least, more repenting.

Anyone who wants to become immortal doesn't

know anything about living forever. Life becomes monotonous, meaningless, when they're forced to relive the same events over and over again with no end. Always the same outcome, always the same result, because no one ever learns. A perpetual cycle, an endless loop.

I used to lie awake at night and wonder about the creatures living outside the realm of Earth, wondering what the species living in other dimensions live like. Wishing, dreaming, that I were one of them, something *other* than human. They always say be careful what you wish for, and they're right. Because now, I'm living that life, and I have regretted it ever since.

My mother always told me not to be afraid, that the creatures I felt wanted to hurt me might actually have something else going on, and might actually need help themselves. A bit like bullies. Sometimes, people hurt others because they're being hurt themselves, and it's their way of dealing with what they're going through.

I didn't believe her; what kid would? I shunned the idea, as all humans do, refusing to trust anyone or anything that might hurt me. I guess this is karma, giving me a taste of my own medicine.

I stand guard, holding my ground as the layer above me continues to shake. The black ground beneath my feet feels softer than usual, like stepping into wet or loose soil, threatening to suck me down into it and never let me go. Never, in the five thousand years of my life down here, have I ever experienced this. I don't remember it *ever* feeling this way, and it strikes me as odd, but I have bigger things to deal with — much more important things. Like my freedom.

I have a mission, and I owe it to my family not to get distracted by something as trivial as the *ground* feeling weird. It's probably nothing, after all.

"Get ready!" I call over my shoulder to my family as they stand behind me, holding hands, alongside other members of our coven.

Any minute now. Any minute, and the ground above us will crack open and reveal the world above our heads, always just out of reach, until now. The doorway to our freedom.

This isn't the first time the door has revealed itself to us; in fact, it's the fourth time that I can recall. Unfortunately, as life would have it, none of the previous times have been successful. Climbing onto the surface and taking back what's rightfully ours isn't as simple as killing a few humans to regain control. Even if we prove victorious, despite many fallen victims, the curse they put on us forces us to remain in these wretched bodies. Without the amulet and the power of the Chosen One, *nothing* we do will ever give us salvation.

The last war was the worst by far. We had such high hopes for the human that we found, the one *obsessed* with my people and the Underworld we are forced to occupy. We should have known that he was blatantly lying to us about being the Chosen One; we should have known better.

He'd constructed his own amulet, convincing us

that it was real, that it would finally set us free. How naïve we were. All our combined years, and we'd let a fake fool us, so desperate for our freedom that we happily believed it was real, purely because we wanted out of our cage.

When the day finally came, when the portal opened, that was when we learned that it was all a lie. The amulet, the Chosen One, all of it was a lie. He'd been studying us for years, learning how we came to be, where we were, and he waited for his chance to prove that he was our king. And when he realized that he wasn't special, that he wasn't *anyone* at all, he had no choice but to lie. So desperate to be something, anything, in a world where he could be a little more than just a maggot.

That lie cost the lives of so many of my own kind, including family members who'd sacrificed themselves for the chance to save the rest. Lives lost for nothing. He didn't survive. Of course, he didn't. Before we were thrown back into the Underworld, we made sure to break his neck to teach him a lesson. It was less than he deserved, but it was all we could do.

This time. This time will be different. This time, *I* will find the Chosen One who can break this curse and save us all. But first, I need to break through this barrier.

"Stand back!" I warn my family.

I have to make sure the coast is clear first. The last thing we need is to breach the surface, only to be ambushed by armed humans waiting to kill us. I can't risk losing anyone else. Not after the loss of my father, not after he sacrificed himself the last time.

It's a tragedy I will always remember. I resent myself for not stepping up, taking his place. I failed him that day, but never again. I will keep the others safe in his memory and make sure no one else dies on my watch. Not if I can help it.

I reach a hand above my head, placing my palm against the concrete as I wait patiently. Or as patiently as I can when all I want to do is free myself of this living hell. I can feel the vibrations through my body, and as soon as I see that first crack of light, I move. I reach for it, fingers curling over the edge of the crack as I pull myself through, leaping out onto the surface and spinning around, motioning for my family to follow me.

The moment my feet touch the black asphalt, I'm struck by the feeling that this was how the ground *used* to feel like in the Underworld, solid and safe. I take a moment to look around. Everything is so different from the last time I was up here, and nothing is as I remember it.

The homes are more developed, stronger than they had been before, and a lot more of them. Made from red brick, an interesting choice. Metal contraptions with wheels cruise along well-paved roads, and large pyramid-shaped poles stick out of the ground, connected with wires from one to the next. The people walking around all carry small devices in their hands, staring at them intently as pictures move upon the faces of the thing they cradle, as if it's their own child.

I breathe a sigh of relief as I finally see something I do recognize. The familiar yellow and purple tones that have plagued my mind for centuries are still prevalent on the streets, despite how strange everything else looks and feels. It's almost comforting, almost, except I know what it means.

Something, other than the homes and how the people are acting, is different this time. Strangely quiet, like an animal waiting to pounce on its prey, leaving the weaker animal terrified of what is inevitable.

It strikes me as being too quiet, and I quickly look back to the doorway, realizing that none of my family members had joined me on the asphalt. The door is sealed shut.

"No, no, no!" I cry, clawing at the place the door had been mere moments ago, hoping to pry it open again and free my friends and family. But it's no use... they're still trapped down there, and I'm alone, left to face the humans alone. What have I done?

"Daddy, look! That man is all black!" I hear a child's voice call out, and I know he's talking about me.

"Kevin, stop that! Don't be rude." The father hisses.

I know what he's thinking, and I don't blame him, but it's not what the kid means.

I dart for the bushes that line the street, hiding out of sight and waiting until the father and son move away, grateful for the man's embarrassment as it means he doesn't want to linger longer than he has to. I look down at the dark skin on my hands, repulsed. I look as though my skin has been covered in oil. Thick, slick, and sickly.

This isn't what we planned. Centuries of organization, and everything has gone wrong; none of this was meant to happen. My family is supposed to be here with me, by my side, finding the Chosen One and destroying the humans. I can't do this alone. I don't have the strength to fight them all by myself.

CHAPTER 2

I hear a whistle, and I whip around, my gaze fixing on a man walking in my direction, alone. I smile. The perfect prey for my disguise, some good luck at last. I check that we're alone; no need to alert anyone as to what I'm about to do... or to the fact that I'm even here. Not yet, anyway.

Confident that we're alone, I lunge at him from behind the bushes, tackling the man to the ground. He screams and cries at my appearance as he struggles to free himself from my grasp, but I'm far stronger than he is, and his struggles are futile. I can see the way he's looking at me, but I can't say he looks much better, with his balding head and the beach ball barely contained by his hideous garments.

"Who are you? Wh-What are you?" He whimpers, eyes wide as he stares at me. "Please, don't hurt me. Someone, anyone, help!" His whining voice scrapes against my skull. For a man who looks like he could be a wrestler, a sumo wrestler anyway, he sure doesn't scream like one.

I try to conceal the disgust and pain that the shrieking tone of his voice causes me. I'm not willing to show any weakness to my prey, but that voice!

Even my little sister sounds less squeaky when she tries to summon an army of the dead, only to have that army turn on her seconds later. I've told her hundreds of times to not conjure an entire army when she can't even manage one hellhound. But she never listens. She has the strongest power out of all of us, but she can't control it.

Melanesia isn't like the rest of us. When the ground swallowed us five millennia ago, we didn't find ourselves alone. We stood in the presence of *real* demons, fire-breathing demons with claws sharp enough to rip open a grown human being and fling him into another universe entirely.

We were terrified and confused at first, faced with these creatures we'd only heard stories about for years, watching as they killed off so many of us. Those of us they spared, they accepted, molding us into their own. We learned to live with them for five thousand years, plotting our next move to take down the humans, but our goals were very different from theirs.

We wanted to redeem ourselves, to reclaim what was rightfully ours, and achieve our salvation. For them, sparing us and helping us was in exchange for our help when they asked for it, though they never did tell us what they wanted, and we didn't really care since all we wanted was to get our lives back.

That was how my sister was born. After my father died during our last attempt to overthrow the humans, my mother chose to remarry. To *him*. I'm not even really sure if demons *have* genders, or the known body parts that usually go with genders, but if any of them do, it's *him*. They're creatures of destruction, with magical abilities to reproduce in ways I've never really understood.

Asmodeus, my step-father, isn't exactly a saint. Other than Lucifer himself, Asmodeus is the most ruthless demon in the Underworld. He has no shame in eradicating anyone who crosses his path, or even looks at him weird. I remember once when one of my own dared to joke around and call him "Lord Ass" rather than "Lord Asmodeus," and I swear, I've never seen anyone liquify so fast before that moment. One snap of his fingers and gone, nothing left but a puddle of red goop that had once been someone I'd known. I learned to fear him, in my own way, and respect him in another.

It wasn't long before Melanesia was born. Half-human, half-demon. Powerful enough to levitate a small town after just one year of training, which is more dangerous than some of the fully-trained half-demons I'd been around. In a way, it's fortunate for this world that my sister still has a lot to learn. But then again, it isn't because we would have been able to beat the humans with ease if she could control her own powers. But we have a long way to go before Melanesia is going to be able to blink an eyelid and wipe humans out in the way her father wants her to.

My fist slams into the man's face, knocking him out cold with one hit. Maybe a little too cold... since he stops breathing immediately. I shrug; I don't care that he's dead.

"One less human to kill later," I mutter, throwing his limp body into the bushes behind me once I remove the items that I need.

Putting on his yellow coat and picking up his purple umbrella, I roll my shoulders until the coat settles on me more comfortably. Hopefully, it will be enough to keep me unnoticed for a little while, until I can figure out how to open the door and let the rest of my kind out and onto the surface.

My family, my entire family, is still trapped in that abyss, and I'd much rather be there with them than here alone in my enemy's territory. It only takes one wrong look from someone, and I'll be as good as dead.

I'm strong. I like to pride myself on that, but without any real powers other than looking like a freak, there's no way I can defend myself on my own, let alone take out the humans. I don't think even Lucifer has the power to take on this town alone, not with the curse. It's why he needs us. I can speak telepathically through dreams, but then again, everyone in the Underworld can. It's how we learned to communicate without Lucifer finding out.

He's a tyrant and a dictator, and most of the conversations involve wishes to overthrow him and take over his kingdom. But sometimes, it's better to suck it up and do his bidding, rather than risk combustion. The phrase "better the devil you know" is pretty accurate. As awful as Lucifer is, we know who, and what, he is, but if someone like my step-father were to take over? Well... who knows what will happen to us?

They're just dreams, wishes that have to remain wishes. After witnessing Eisheth, one of Lucifer's own, betray him like Judas betrayed Jesus, none of us dare go against Lucifer ever again.

I'll never forget that night when Lucifer discovered Eisheth's betrayal, the image of Eisheth's body incinerating under the raging inferno of Lucifer's flames, his eyeballs melting down his face. One minute he was there, and the next, a pile of ashes. It lasted minutes, in reality, but it felt as though hours had passed, and we were all scared.

But what good is dream telepathy, anyway? Hop into the dreams of my family, apologize for being a dick and leaving them all behind? I'm sure they'll all love that. I'm sure that would make up for the fact that I'm here, and they're not. As much as I hate my step-father, I wish I have the power that Asmodeus does. One evil stare, and the person he's looking at vanishes into nothingness, as though they were never there to begin with.

The rain is coming down hard and fast now, and I wonder how the humans deal with the constant wetness of their world, the cold that bites right into your very soul. Where I'm from, I know only heat. Hot and dry. That's it. I've been down there for so long that I barely remember what fresh air feels like. It's not the cleanest smell, but it's refreshing compared to the stench of death and decay that's suffocated me for longer than I dare admit.

I look down at my hands, like pools of the night sky giving form. All I can think about is that if I ever get my original skin back, I'm never complaining about being pale ever again.

I pull up the collar of the yellow coat and lower my head, pulling the umbrella down low so I can keep my face as hidden from others' view as much as possible. Given the strength of the rain, I'll be surprised if anyone can see my face well enough to notice the color of my skin, but I don't want to risk it, either.

"Howdy!" Suddenly, a man calls out to me in a jovial tone.

I automatically turn my head in his direction, twitching the collar again to ensure that the lower half of my face is covered by the yellow coat. The man is wearing a coat just like mine, and he carries the same purple umbrella. He waves at me with a smile, his round belly jiggling as he hurries along the path.

"It's really coming down out here! Best be heading home; don't want to get blown away now, do you?" He laughs to himself, and all I can do is roll my eyes.

"Yeah, sure." I force a chuckle from my throat, glancing back at the pavement rather than looking at him.

"My wife warned me about coming out on a day like this, but I couldn't help but run to the store for a six pack. You get it, us men and our needs." He chuckles, continuing to talk despite my clear disinterest.

If these humans didn't have weapons, their constant chatter and grating voices would be the death of me.

"You seem like you can use some cheering up, my friend. Care for a beer? I can survive on five for one night!" The man laughs again, his cackle beginning to make my brain bleed.

I finally look up at him and see that he's holding out a bottle with a strange yellow liquid inside. I catch his smile, so wholesome, so innocent, that for a moment, I almost forget that these humans are killers. I shake my head at him, rejecting his offer, but the smile remains on his face.

I don't want to be here. Not without my family.

I'm not here to make friends; I'm here for revenge.

"Suit yourself!" he replies in a sing-song voice. "But if you change your mind about that beer or get hungry, there's a great pub just a street down. I go there all the time." My eyes follow where the man points down the road toward the direction he'd just come from, and I look over my shoulder out of courtesy, trying not to draw attention to myself.

"Thanks," I mutter, watching the jolly plump man skip away.

My stomach begins to growl, and I silently curse him for mentioning food. In the Underworld, the demons eat — they eat my kind, humans turned into monsters, who look more threatening than we really are. The reality is, we can't really defend ourselves, not really. It's why they pick us off, feeding their greedy, hungry bellies out of spite more than necessity, keeping us afraid so we remember our place.

The rest of us are left with the colorless gruel they serve the animals down there, twisted creatures that would just as readily eat us as the demons would. Thick gray gruel that looks and tastes like concrete — hard enough to kill someone if thrown at them. I don't even dare imagine what it's made from; I've never been brave enough to ask. I found the bone of a finger in it once, but I don't like to think about it for too long, or else it makes me feel sick.

Maybe eating something isn't a bad idea after all. I'm weak and lightheaded, tend I'm alone in this world without the strength and support of my friends and family. I need to regain what little strength I have remaining. If they do attack, I don't have enough in me to fight back, and I have to stay alive. I have to stay safe for the sake of my family.

I have to make this right, and to do that, I have to find the Chosen One.

I turn around and stroll back down the way the man had pointed, keeping my head down to shield myself from the rain and keep my face hidden from all the other humans in yellow coats who glance in my direction. I don't know whether it's just paranoia, or whether they *are* all staring at me.

What the hell is so fascinating, anyway? I look just like everybody else in this godforsaken town — yellow and purple, my most hated colors in the whole universe. They're lucky I'm not my step-father. One look from him, and they'll all be gone. For good.

My stomach growls angrily at me the further down the road I get, so much so that I'm sure the people around me can hear it. The last thing I need is my stomach drawing attention to my presence. It's difficult enough to hide in plain sight as it is.

I clutch at my stomach as I continue down the road, searching for this infamous pub the man had been yammering about. I don't know what a beer is, but I'll happily take a bowl of barley and a glass of warm cow's milk. It's simple, and most would refer to it as "peasant" food, but to me, it would be the best meal in the whole world right now. *Anything* has to be better than the gray gruel I've been eating for the last thousand years.

I have no idea what this pub looks like. It's not a word I understand, but after a moment or two longer, a fragrant aroma wafts my way across the damp wind, and my stomach immediately answers with another, much louder, rumble. I stop, bending over slightly as I attempt to ignore the cramping in my belly, looking up at the sign above the door.

"Ge... Gera?" I try to make it out. "Whatever." What does it even matter? I don't even care; I just need food.

I don't want to hesitate. I don't want to show any sign of weakness, but at the same time, I'm afraid I'll be spotted and ambushed. As my stomach screams at me to fill it, I know I can't put it off anymore. I need to fill it, or I'll collapse from hunger, and then what will happen when they find me unconscious on the floor? Easy pickings for the enemy.

Driven inside by my need to stuff my face, the smell hits me hard. The delicious aroma mixes with something reminiscent of century-old wheat that's been left out to dry... and then rot in the sun. It reminds me of before, of home. It might not be the most pleasant smell, or the most pleasant memory, but it's more familiar than anything else in this world so far, and I cling to that.

"What can I get for you?" The man who speaks to me is scruffy, with wide blue eyes and a nose large enough that it feels like if he turned around too quickly, he would knock someone out with it. He nods his head at me as he wipes his pudgy, hairy hands on the dirty fabric around his waist, pulling a cloth from the pocket of the garment as he begins wiping down the surface in front of me. He then picks up the silver domes on the side and brushes away the crumbs from underneath them.

"Uh..." I hesitate, unsure of what to say, let alone what to ask for. I'm reminded of how different things are now since the last time my kind managed to reach the surface. I know nothing of this world. Keeping myself hidden is going to be difficult at the best of times, but it feels almost impossible right now.

"What? You gotta speak up, buddy. It's way too loud in here to be murmuring, and I'm hard of hearing." The man grunts at me, tapping at his ear.

"Ca-Can I get some food?" I ask stiffly, still keeping my voice low as though I expect the whole place to turn and stare at me if they hear me speak too loudly.

"Yeah, well, we got plenty of that here. What do you want? Burger? Cheesesteak? Fries? What?" he asks.

Burger? Cheesesteak? Fries? I don't recognize any of these words, but they don't sound like food to me. Before our incarceration, back when I was still a full human, I'd gotten used to the simple meals of barley, wheat, and what little I could manage to hunt with my own bare hands. I have no idea what a burger is. I have no idea if it's even alive or a plant. It's all completely new to me.

"Can I get a bowl of barley, please? And a glass of warm milk?" I ask, keeping my head low as I sit at the counter. My shoulders are slouched, and the hood of the yellow coat is pulled up over my head.

"Dude, what the hell are you talkin' about? This is

a pub, not a farm. We ain't got none of that shit here. You want a burger or not?" the man asks angrily.

"Is... it is alive?"

The man laughs, patting his huge belly with a hand. "Ha! I hope not. Otherwise, I might have a lawsuit on my hands!" Suddenly, his smile turns into a scowl, and his eyebrows furrow as he stares at me. "Don't tell me you're one of those fucking vegans. All these Angelenos, always coming into my bar on their way to some dumbass festival or other lame event, asking for fucking tofu cheesesteaks and po-po bowls, or whatever is trending down there. Sick to death of it! Nothing wrong with a good bit of meat!"

I shake my head quickly, not wanting to draw any more attention to myself. I don't understand a word the man is saying, but as his cheeks turn red, I recognize human anger and realize it's best just to agree with him rather than make him angrier. If I ask any more questions, I'm only going to attract the attention of everyone else inside this stinky place, and I have to stay hidden for as long as I can.

"Good. Burger, then?" The man smiles again, his anger forgotten, and I'm just grateful that whatever response I'd given him is the right one.

I nod, hoping that this "burger" is going to be enough to fill my aching stomach. I need to figure this new world out quickly so that I can fit in and hide until I can bring my family to me.

"One heart attack burger comin' right up! I swear, you haven't had a real burger until you've had a

Geraldy's famous heart attack burger." The man leans in closer. "The secret is ten strips of the fattiest bacon you can find." He chuckles. "Little advice, buddy. Lay off the sunbeds. I don't know what kinda crazy voodoo pigment you got goin' on there, but I ain't ever seen that color on a man before." He laughs heartily.

I scowl slightly, shrinking under his gaze and pulling the coat tighter around me. Congratulations, Draven, as if this stupid yellow coat is ever going to be enough to hide me from the humans' sight. Nothing is *ever* going to be enough to conceal the monster that I am. Though, he hasn't immediately reached for a carving knife, so I should be glad of that small stroke of luck, I suppose.

My stomach continues to growl as he leaves me, and I take the opportunity to look around the room. It's noisy, despite there only being four to five humans in here, along with myself and the scruffy man. They don't look like the humans I remember, the ones who attacked and killed my father on sight. *They* had murder in their eyes, stern and evil; *they* were ready to kill us.

But these humans? These ones are insane; they're loopier than Asmodeus when he's had one chalice of blood too many. These humans, laughing and drinking something I don't recognize in excess, they're disconnected from reality in a way I don't understand. I wonder if these humans would even be able to destroy us demons; they're not at all like I remember them.

"Here you go, buddy. Your burger." The scruffy

man returns and puts a fragrant round monstrosity down in front of me, pulling my attention away from these clowns I'm meant to be afraid of.

I turn my attention to the soft, spherical object, its delicious smell enticing me toward it, filling my brain with my hunger as I stare at this unusual thing in front of me. I reach out a finger and poke the top of it, smiling as it squishes down under the pressure of my finger.

"Heh. Squishy," I mutter. "Of course, it is. I'd break my teeth otherwise." I roll my eyes at myself, wondering how I even manage to function some days.

The scruffy man snorts in amusement, raising an eyebrow at me as he watches me interact with my burger. "What's the matter? Never seen a burger before?" he asks me.

I shake my head, suddenly feeling very conscious of that fact. Clearly, it's an odd thing not to have had, which only makes me stick out like a sore thumb.

"You know, you're a very, very peculiar man. Skin dark as ash, walkin' around in a daze, asking for barley and milk. You're definitely not from around here, but I like it, and I've decided that I like you." He chuckles, pointing to the burger still squished underneath my finger. "Try it. You'll love it; trust me."

I reach down to take the burger in my hands, watching as its juices drip down onto the plate below, the smell making my mouth water. Licking my lips, I take a large bite out of the soft thing, flavor flooding my tongue as my saliva fills my mouth at the delectable taste. I swallow and let out a soft moan of pleasure as I smile at the man.

"Like it?" he asks, though I can tell by his face that he already knows the answer.

"This is the best thing I have ever tasted in my life," I reply with a nod.

"Knew you'd like it; everyone always does. Unless they're one of those stupid vegans." He snorts. "Don't got no business being in my life if you don't like burgers." He adds with a nod. "Tell ya what, seein' as this is the first time you've had one, it's on the house."

"On the house?" I ask, not understanding why the burger would be on the house.

He laughs and claps a hand on his belly. "You really are something, you know that? On the house! Free of charge! You just enjoy that, and don't worry about havin' to pay me." He smiles.

My face feels hot as my cheeks flush red. I feel like such an idiot, though I'm grateful the man finds my clear naivety amusing rather than irritating. I know absolutely nothing of what the world is now, and it's evident to this man, as well as to me.

These people are idiots, all of them. I can't believe my luck; I'd expected to spend my time running and hiding, fighting for my life, but these people are oblivious to what I really am. They don't see me as a threat at all, and that's going to work out in my favor.

I can't let my true colors show, not just yet, but at least it's doubtful that these fools will even realize who or what I am, too dumb to realize what they're looking at or why I don't understand their simple phrases. I can't forget my mission, either. There's too much at stake, and my family needs me.

I stay at the pub for an hour or so, letting the scruffy man chat me up while he's still happy to do so, and while he's content to feed me free food, having discovered that I know very little of their cuisine. It took a little stretching of the truth for him to understand that "where I came from," we ate very plain foods, and that such exotic meals are foreign to me.

He seems nice enough, but I'm also not naïve enough to believe that he won't turn on me the moment he realizes what I am. For the brief moment that he's useful, he's fueling me and helping me regain my strength. He's also teaching me a little more about this world, but beyond that, he'll still end up dying by my hands when the time comes.

After leaving the pub, I spend several hours wandering around the streets, looking for signs of something I'm not even sure exists anymore. I'm drained and ready to give up, the strain of being alone weighing heavily upon me as I walk these unfamiliar streets alone. My family has always been my backbone, my support system, and without them, I feel utterly lost.

Knowing that they're trapped down there, that they couldn't get out when I did, tears at my heart, and I feel nauseous. The food I had just eaten churns in my stomach at the thought of my family clawing at the ground above their heads, trying to join me here on the surface.

Everywhere I go, I'm surrounded by yellow coats and purple umbrellas, each person passing me by with either a smile or a look of disgust, but none of the hatred I expected to find when I pulled myself free from the Underworld. I'm not sure which look I prefer from these humans, the disgust or the absurd smile.

I look up at the sky as I stand on a gross knoll beneath the trees, the rain splattering across my face. It's growing dark now, the day finally turning to night, a chance for me to blend in, thanks to my dark skin. The moon and stars shine above me, glowing brightly in a way I'd almost forgotten, so used to the cavernous hell of molten lava that had been home for the last few millennia.

The cold wind beats the rain down hard on me, and I shiver as it grips my skin with its icy fingers. I haven't felt cold in so long that I'd forgotten what it feels like. It feels so peaceful out here, beautiful in its own way, making me feel as though my life is a little less chaotic...

CHAPTER 3

"Draven! Draven!" I wake up to the sound of my sister's voice screaming my name, dragging me from the deep slumber I'd finally managed to get into.

"Huh?" I whisper as I stir, blinking and looking around myself, still on the grassy knoll beneath the trees where I had stopped to look at the night sky above me. It's still dark, and I look around frantically, finding nothing but the tree branches blowing in the wind, and the large drops of rain still falling from the sky.

"Melanesia? Is that you? Where are you?" I call out to her, my heart pounding in my chest as I try to see where she's hiding, searching for a shadowy figure that could be my sister.

"Up here, sweetie," another voice calls me, calmer and more mature, "look up."

My eyes dart to the sky above me, filled with stars and dark clouds, my mother and sister smiling down at me and waving.

"Mom? Melanesia?"

"Yes, sweetie, it's us. We're here. We came to check on you, to make sure you're safe." My mother replies in her soft, loving tone, making my heart ache as all I want to do is hold her.

"What happened?" I ask, forcing myself not to cry or show her any fear — I don't want her to worry any more than she probably already has been. "Why didn't the rest of you follow me?"

"We tried, sweetheart, we tried. But everyone was pushing us. They created a block in the doorway, and by the time any of us could get free enough to pull ourselves through, the doorway had closed on us. It didn't stay open as long as it usually does," my mother replies, a sadness in her tone.

"Yeah, why'd you run off so fast, Draven? Mother was afraid the humans would just murder you at first sight. I'm surprised you're still alive," Melanesia chimes in cheerfully. She's still young and somewhat naïve, and still finds death and destruction fascinating — she truly is her father's daughter in that respect. There's less of my mother in her than there is Asmodeus, and it's terrifying.

"Melanesia, stop that!" my mother snaps at her, chiding her daughter.

"Sorry," my sister whispers.

I still find it miraculous that my sister will listen to anyone other than her father, given the power that she holds, but she seems to love and respect our mother enough to behave herself when told. Though, I don't know how long that will last, not once my sister figures out how to control her powers, and she realizes that she doesn't really need to listen to mother at all.

My eyes meet my mother's, and I can see the relief on her face. Like Melanesia said, mother had been worried. I feel a little better knowing that she clearly doesn't hate me for getting out while they're all still stuck in the Underworld. I'm just glad she can reach out to me this way.

"I'm glad you're okay, but there's no turning back now. You know that, don't you? The surface won't open for us again until you find the Chosen One, sweetheart. Whoever that may be. You have to find them, Draven, and reopen the portal for us all to follow you, Otherwise, I'm afraid you're stuck up there without us, separated for another thousand years until the portal opens again on its own."

"What about Lucifer? I'm sure *he* has the power to crack the surface." It's a question we've all wanted to ask but never quite dared to. However, now that I'm alone, he can't do me any harm for speaking out against him *unless* he comes up here to give me a lesson. And if he does, the others can follow him. Win-win.

My mother shakes her head, looking sad again. "No, not even Lucifer has the power to manipulate the portal that separates the Earth and the Underworld. Otherwise, he would have marched his armies against the humans long ago. It's up to you, Draven. I know it's a lot to ask of you, but we all believe in you. Jeziah says the Chosen One will be a green-eyed belle who wears a pentagram ring. Find her, sweetie. Find her, and save us all."

"Yeah, Draven. Don't fuck it up." Melanesia snaps at me, wincing as mother glares at her for swearing. "You're our only hope," she adds in a slightly less bossy tone.

"Geez, thanks. No pressure, then," I mutter, watching as the vision of my mother and sister wavers and vanishes from the sky, leaving me all alone once again. I should never have expected any compassion from my sister; it had never been her strength. It's not her fault, being what she is. Her empathy is pretty stunted. It never really existed for the demons, and unfortunately, the human half from my mother is tainted by our current situation... not that I think it would have made much difference where Melanesia is concerned.

With my family gone again, I sigh, shivering in the wind and the rain as the cold seeps back in without the distraction that my family's presence offered for a moment. I wrap my arms around myself as I try to stop the shivering, but it's no use; I'm soaked. I never thought I'd miss the heat from the Underworld, and all those things I loathed when I was stuck in that place, the familiarity, the understanding.

Now I'm cold and alone, acutely aware that if I die here from freezing to death, that my family will never get out this time and will face another thousand years trapped beneath the surface, clawing at the black ground above their heads.

I pull myself to my feet and slip down the grassy hill, hugging the purple umbrella close over my head, though at this point, it feels superfluous as I'm already wet. I run, in no particular direction, until I find myself staring at the face of a mountain, its surface pockmarked with more crevices and scars than I have on my entire body. I need to find shelter, and the nooks and caves on the surface are perfect for what I need. I pick the nearest one and rush inside.

The ground below my feet is soft, the soil squishy, reminding me again of how the ground in the Underworld had felt before I escaped. It's empty, except for a couple of squeaking rats, but I don't mind sharing my space with them. At least, I'm not alone. It's warm and dry, and for now, it's sheltered and will suffice until the morning.

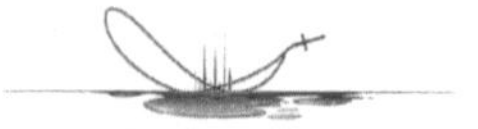

"Draven! Draven, please, don't leave us! Don't leave us!" My mother is crying behind me, but I'm too far ahead to turn back now. If I do, it's all for nothing.

"They're killing us! Brother, help us!" Melanesia's cries are like a dagger to my heart, her fear setting my teeth on edge.

Her desperation causes me to turn around, and I reach my hand out to her, but my hand is rebuffed by a transparent barrier, separating me from my family all over again. I watch in despair as the humans tear into my family, stabbing them with swords, blood and gore dripping from the ends of their blades as they slice my mother's head clean from her shoulders. I'm so close, yet too far away, unable to help, frozen in horror as I watch my family die, crying hard as I collapse to my knees, rocking back and forth as I bite back the rising nausea.

Melanesia emerges from the massacre, her eyes black, bloodied voids where her eyeballs should have been, blood dripping down her cheeks like red tears of despair. "You left us, brother. You left us here to die; it's all your fault!"

"No!" I scream, waking up from my nightmare in a sweat, my heart pounding painfully in my chest as I gasp for breath. I'm alive, and so are they. I know it deep down, but that horrible nightmare lingers in my mind, the image of my family covered in blood harassing me the moment I close my eyes.

I stumble to my feet, leaning heavily against the cold cave wall to support my weight as my legs tremble beneath me, threatening to send me crashing to the floor again. I grab the yellow coat from the rock where I'd left it the previous night to dry, clutching at the umbrella with a trembling hand, willing my fingers not to lose their grip.

I can focus on the small things. I can do this to ground myself, to diminish the images of a fate that I fear more than anything else.

Staggering from the cave, I gasp, gulping in huge breaths of fresh air as the rain slaps against my exposed face. It's still pouring down. I'm not surprised, but I'm not happy about it, either. I'd considered going down to the canal I spotted on my way to the mountain and splashing water on my face, but it's unnecessary with the endless rain. Dark clouds loom overhead, the rain-drops like heavy, wet bullets as they pound against the ground and anything in their way, me included.

There's no sun, and I have no clue what time it is, but I also don't care. All I can think about is finding the Chosen One and saving my family. That's all that matters now — they're counting on me, but every second without knowing who the Chosen One is, feels like a knife to the heart, and the despair I feel at being alone dares to creep back in again.

I make my way to the canal anyway, my mind so

full of my family that my father creeps into my thoughts, and I remember the days spent skipping rocks across the water with him, happy with the simple joy of counting how many skips each we managed to get, counting the ripples that were made when we threw the bigger rocks into the depths of the water.

Nature has always fascinated me, but in all this rain, I'm losing count of the ripples as each raindrop casts their own rings across the turbulent surface of the canal.

As I reach the water's edge, I realize that I'm not as alone as I first thought I was. A girl, wearing a white top and blue bottoms, leans back into the dense puddle behind her without a care in the world, as though she doesn't even realize it's raining at all. She's soaked, her top clinging to her skin, her brown hair dangling behind her in wet strands that nearly touch the ground.

The sight of her makes my cheeks flush, but I doubt anyone could see the color against my dark skin. And my eyes. My eyes are drawn to the hard nubs of her nipples, pressing against her top in the cold, damp weather. It's been so long since I've seen anyone so beautiful, and the way she doesn't care attracts me immediately and without reason.

Love is meaningless to my people. My mother married Asmodeus out of the pure need to survive, not out of affection — but as I gaze upon this woman, I have a vague recollection of what romance was from when I was still human, what it feels to be attracted to someone for reasons other than to survive.

I'm drawn to her, fascinated as she picks up a rock and tosses it into the water in front of her, watching the ripples, just as I had been. I think I love her already, this beautiful creature before me. I want to see her face, but I'm afraid of her seeing me for what I really am — she's human; she'll kill me on the spot. Though so far, none of the others have, but the fear remains, especially after my nightmares.

I hear her move, and I dive behind a bush, hiding in the foliage as she gets up and starts to walk away. As she moves closer to me, she reaches into her backpack, but that's not what catches my eye. It's the flash of something on her finger... and then I see it.

The ring. The *pentagram* ring. She looks toward my direction, and I catch sight of her eyes for the first time — deep emeralds that glisten even in this darkness. She's the Chosen One! I've found her!

I knew there was something special about her! What other person would be out in this weather without a coat or an umbrella? Unlike the rest of this strange town, she's not sporting the yellow coat and purple umbrella that seem to be almost required by the residents, and like me, I feel like she doesn't belong here anymore than I do. It's meant to be; it's fate.

My heart races so loudly in my chest that I'm afraid she might hear it, but she doesn't, walking alone in the rain and vanishing around the corner. Oblivious to my existence. I don't question it, for now I'm grateful.

I have to be cautious, however. I have to take things

slow and get her on my side. As much as I want to grab her and beg her to help my family, I know that this could drive her further away and lead to my death... and then what? Another thousand years of waiting for my family because I'd been too impatient to coax the Chosen One to our side?

Keeping my distance, I follow her, determined to keep my eye on her. I can't lose her. I need to make sure I know where she is so that I can start to bring her around to our side, to make her see that what's been done to us is unfair. She never even looks back, never suspects that someone's following her, but why would she? Out here, in this sea of yellow coats and purple umbrellas, *she* is the odd one out, not me. I've got my disguise, pathetic as it may be, but it's enough to protect me from any immediate scrutiny, and it lets me blend in enough that she doesn't even bother to look back at me.

Once she's home, I wait, listening to the voices inside the home, keeping as still and hidden as I can until I know where she is. Despite the cold, despite the rain, I pull off the yellow coat and flatten the umbrella, hiding them in one of the garden bushes, ready to retrieve them if, and when, I need to. For now, my dark skin is my camouflage. I may hate it, but it's useful for the time being.

A voice, feminine and melodic, drifts from one of the back windows, and I hurry around the side of the house, pulling myself up the lattice fence that's nailed onto the side with ease until I'm at her window ledge, protected from the rain by the roof, able to sit and listen as I blend into the shadows of the house under the darkened sky.

I can't hear who she's talking to, but I can hear her side of things, enough to know that she's talking to a boy and that her name is Bella Nova. I instantly hate him. Millennia of hatred for humans boiling over and spilling into a grudge against the boy at the other end of that conversation, despite him not being in the room with her. I know she's not mad; she's holding one of those silly objects I'd seen when I first arrived to her head and talking into it, though I don't really understand what it is. He's my rival, though he doesn't yet know it.

My heart aches in my chest as I see her smiling from her bed, and all I want to do is reach out and touch her, wondering what it would feel like to kiss her lips. Her eyes glitter like emeralds, and I'm jealous of the boy she's so happily enjoying a conversation with. He's not a man, not in my eyes. If he were, he would have been here in person to say whatever sweet nothings he's uttering to her through the strange device. Only a coward would say such things from afar.

I shiver, wishing I had some warmer clothing to wear, but the coat is too bright, and she would surely see me if I were to wear it while I watched her. I need to know more about her, need to be closer to her and understand who she is. I need to make her understand that she's our only hope of ever reclaiming what's rightfully ours.

I wait for her to fall asleep, knowing that my best chance to interact with her is through dream telepathy. It's the easiest way to speak without her immediately threatening my life, and this way, I can know her innermost thoughts as well. Her dreams are restless, and I realize what I'm watching is a memory, rather than a nightmare that her mind has made up — the details are too clear, too precise to be a dream.

I see the man hurting her, and I want to step forward and tear him apart. I need her, in more ways than one, and I cannot afford for him to hurt her — but I can't do anything. This has already happened, but at least I know about it.

Seconds before she wakes up, I feel a thought drift across her mind, that she wishes the memories would go away, even for a moment, and I smile to myself. That's my window; that's how I reach her. I steal those dreams from her and replace them with my own.

Bella Nova, you will be mine.

I CHOOSE to sleep during the day, leaving Bella to go about her day while I rest and get my head back on straight. I settle back into my cave and concentrate on my breathing, closing my eyes and drifting off, reaching out to my family as I do so.

The Underworld is a cavernous place of black rock, sharp and porous like lava cooling over time, though there are still rivers of lava glowing throughout the entire place, the black ground of the layer above us like a perpetual night sky. I've spent millennia dreaming about getting out of this place, and now that I'm standing here, a dream-self, all I want is to be back with my family in the stifling heat.

"Draven!" My mother's voice calls to me as she sees me standing close by, and she hurries to me with Melanesia beside her. "What's wrong?"

"I've found her. I've found the Chosen One."

"Then why are you *here*?" Melanesia rolls her eyes at me, arms crossed over her chest as she gives me her best glare, much like Asmodeus would... though if it were him, I'd be dead.

"To *tell* you that I've found her." I roll my eyes at her in return. "I'm going to work on her tonight. I'll get her on our side. I just wanted to let you know."

"Be quick, sweetie. I don't like you being up there all on your own."

I smile and nod, but I say nothing else. I know I'm alone. I don't need reminding, and I certainly don't want to think about it. I also don't want to think about how long it might take me to get Bella on our side either, but I can only do what I can do.

I leave the dream behind and rest, waking up and making my way back down the mountain and into town under the cover of night. It's time. I climb up the lattice fence to Bella's window, smiling at her sleeping face as I reach out to her dreams like I did the night before, inserting myself into them this time.

"Bella, Bella Nova," I call to her softly in her dream.

"What? Who is it? Who's here?" she replies.

I can hear the fear in her voice, but I need her. I need her to listen.

The world around us reflects the only world I've known for the last five millennia, the world of the Underworld, all black and red and full of nightmares that she can't possibly imagine.

"Hello?" she calls out to me again in an uncertain tone, wary, afraid, but I don't have time to be gentle or kind — I need her now.

She looks around, but she doesn't see me, and I fear that she's unable to see me, that my connection isn't strong enough. She starts to walk away from me, and my heart leaps into my chest as I reach out to her, our connection growing weaker.

"Bella, Bella!" My voice is drowned out by another, and she's pulled away from me.

Dragged from the dream, I open my eyes and quietly curse as her mother shakes her awake. I don't have time to waste. I'm going to have to be more aggressive in my approach if I want to get her to listen to me. My family is counting on me. I cannot waste any more time.

CHAPTER 4

Watching him kiss her, I imagine what it would feel like to rip his head straight off from his shoulders, but I know better. There's no point in killing him, not yet anyway, not in front of Bella. I need her on my side, and killing her *precious* boyfriend would only turn her against me entirely. He can have today, can spend it with her and touch her, but he won't get anymore. After tonight, I intend to make her mine, and I won't stop until she is.

I return back to my cave for the day after stopping at the pub for a quick meal with my strange new friend, the man who owns the place. He seems to have taken a liking to me, or he pities me. Whichever it is, I don't care. He feeds me for nothing, and I'm not going to scoff at that.

He looks at me, but I don't think he *sees* me. I don't think any of them do. It's as if they're oblivious to what I really am. Either that, or their inability to believe in our kind has left them blind to what's staring them straight in the face.

Whatever the reason, I don't care. It means I can move a little more freely and without worry, as these ignorant humans genuinely seem unaware of what now walks amongst them. If my family were here, we could have defeated these weak fools with ease, but on my own... the minute I dare to try could be my undoing. I'm alone here, and while I *could* take them on, they would begin to fight back. What use would I be to my family then?

I dream of my family while I sleep, nightmares that wake me violently and leave me drenched in sweat, the faces of my family imprinted in my memory and on my eyes, even as I stare at the blank cave wall, gasping for breath as the sweat beads down my back. It's always the same dream. My failure resulting in my family being stuck in the Underworld for another millennia, or them getting to the surface and being slaughtered while all I can do is watch helplessly. I refuse to let my dreams become reality. I can't let that happen to my family. They're already suffering because of me, and I can't let them down again.

Dragging myself from my current shelter, I make my way back to Bella's home, my heart calling me to her window, instinctively drawn to her very existence. I watch as she kisses the corsage that *he* clearly gave her, and I instantly want to tear it to shreds with my hands. He has her heart at the moment, but it won't last; I'll make sure of it. Soon, she will be mine, and he will be nothing but a distant memory. A bad smell she wishes to forget. How could she ever want him over me?

I want her to slip into bed, to go to sleep so that I can join her in her dream. It's as close to her as I can be right now, but anything is better than nothing until I can persuade her to help me and my family. I watch her bend over her desk, working on something I don't truly understand, let alone remotely care about.

"Please, Bella, I need you to sleep. I need you to see me," I whisper quietly, my breath fogging up her window as I watch her longingly.

All I want to do is gather her in my arms and kiss her, taste her on my lips. The thought of her body pressed against mine arouses me, and I groan softly at the thought of her bare skin against mine. I shift comfortably, my cock pressing hard against my bottoms. I've not felt like this for over five thousand years, not felt the call of my sexual instincts, let alone met anyone who has brought them to the surface like she does. I know it's stupid and dangerous to let her distract me, but I can't think of anything else as I watch her breathe slowly, her shoulders shifting gently with the movement as she works.

I want to take her by her shoulders, spin her around, and kiss her in such a way that she fears I may devour her in my need to touch her. I wouldn't, but the growing need in my heart and bottoms would suggest otherwise.

Finally, she rises from her chair, giving me a welcoming distraction from the tingling sensation in my groin that aches to be satiated. I watch her with eager eyes as she collapses onto her bed, asleep the instant her head hits the soft pillow, and I know that it's my chance at last. *My* chance to be with her. I close my eyes and will my racing heart to slow its pace. The vigorous drumbeat is too distracting for what I need to do. I close my eyes and picture her face, her dreams, like I did before, until I wake up to find myself in the shadows of her mind.

"Bella, Bella Nova," I call to her, almost shocked by the deep, reverberating sound of my own voice as though I've forgotten what I sound like. I try not to be nervous about being close to her, but I can't help it. I love her. I *need* her.

I hear her cry out in pain and immediately want to rush to her, pull her into my arms and keep her close and safe. I know I can't approach her, not yet. I need her to seek *me* out. So, when she does, when she tells me to show myself and stop playing games, I do as she asks, sort of. Hands clenched into fists to stop myself from trembling, I turn a corner behind a large boulder. I *know* she will follow me because, of course, she will. She wants answers, and I want her to want me.

She does exactly as I expect her to, running around the boulder, thinking I'm waiting there. But of course, I'm not. I need her to keep chasing me. The more I'm a mystery, the more she will want me.

I can feel her frustration as she finds that I'm not there waiting for her as she'd expected, and I can't help but smile, my heart pounding in my chest again as I wait for her to realize that I'm actually behind her. Finally, she sees me, *me*, all of me as I truly am. It shouldn't hurt as much as it does when she yelps and steps away from me, her eyes wide and filled with fear at the sight of the monster I am because of a simple and arrogant mistake I made long ago.

Lost in her eyes, I lose my voice, forgetting how to speak as I stare into the deep, green pools staring back at me. Finally, she speaks, and it's like music to my ears because she's talking to *me*. I feel as though I might float away with happiness that she can finally see me, that I'm the one who has her attention... until she says *his* name. I'm not angry with her. I don't think I can be, but I feel as though her fingers are digging into my heart and ripping it into two.

I step toward her and reach out on impulse, my

hand resting against her cheek, freezing there as I feel her warmth under my fingers, but as she says his name again, I shake my head, swallowing the hurt and my pride. It's time, time to make her mine.

"My name is Draven Asmodeus. I am a demon of the Underworld, and I need your help."

She whispers the word "Hell," and then she's gone from the dream, from my grasp, and even as I reach for her, I know I'll have to try again. Time is running out for my family, and I need to make Bella understand. I need her to work with me so that I can save them. But everything hinges on her. Everything.

I gasp as I return to the waking world, watching her leave her room and return again a moment later to go back to sleep. She's exhausted, and so am I. Pushing my intention, my need, on her is tiring, even for such short periods of time, and I know I'm getting desperate. I have to try harder.

Tomorrow night. Tomorrow night, I *have* to make her understand. I can still feel her on my hand, where my fingertips stroked her cheek, and I moan softly at the thought of touching the rest of her skin, of hearing *her* moan with pleasure because of *me*. I have to stay close to her. I need her as much as I need to breathe. I can't fail again. I need to make her see me.

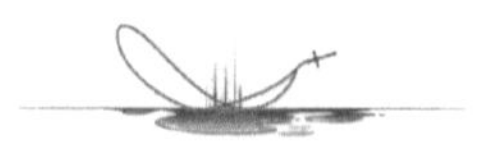

I CAN BARELY SLEEP during the day, Bella haunting my every thought, replacing the nightmarish images of my family being slaughtered with the far sweeter image of her in my arms. She left me restless, wanting more, longing for the dream to become a reality. The erection pressing against my clothes is uncomfortable and aches for release, but I know I have to wait. Not that it stops me from dreaming of her again, naked and sweating beneath me as I slide into her and feel her writhe against my body.

When I return to her house, this time, I'm reminded of those dreams, of the way her skin felt against my hand the night before, and the feeling of her naked body pressed against mine, the electric tingle my imagination came up with that I'm convinced was real. I want her; I need her. The more I think about it, the more I love her.

Focus! I hiss to myself. I'm so caught up in what I want that I can't focus on what I need to do. *He's* there with her, courting her in the way that I should be, and it gives me something to cling to. Hatred is a powerful emotion, one that demons are more than a little familiar with. Asmodeus taught us all how to use our anger and hatred, concentrating on it in order to strengthen ourselves and our powers. That's what I need to remember. I need to hate the other boy for being the one she sees right now. I need to hate the humans for what they did to my family, and I need to make Bella see me.

I take a deep breath and close my eyes, staying

close to Bella in her dream and watching as the boy smiles at her. The fire in my heart is kindled by that look, a raging inferno that, one day, I swear will burn him from the Earth the moment my family is free. Bella will be mine, and he will become nothing but a speck of dust in the wind.

With the ball of hatred now a painful fist around my heart, I know it's time, time to reach across the dream and break the barrier. I need Bella to hear me this time. I was so close last time, but I *have* to make her understand how important she is, more so than this idiotic human brat can ever understand.

"HELP ME!" I scream, the box that Bella's in shaking around her with the force of my voice and my intention, my desperation for her to hear *me* over him. I hear her call out his name in fear, but I don't care. I'm not going to fail this time. This time, she is *going* to hear me, and she is *going* to see me.

My heart pounds in my chest as I force myself into her dream. I claw my way into his place, melting him, turning him to ash — a foreshadowing of exactly what I'm going to do to him once Bella is on our side, once the Chosen One is mine. This dream? This perfect fantasy of hers? I tear it away and show her the help-less, burning nightmare my family suffers with every day of their lives because of *one* mistake.

We all get told that we get a second chance, a chance where we can redeem ourselves for whatever wrongs we did in our past. But *we* never got that chance. *I* never got that chance, so now I'm taking it.

I stand there on the burning asphalt I've called home for five thousand years, but not by choice. I hate bringing her here as much as I hate that this is where my family is trapped, but I need Bella to understand. I need her to *see* what is happening to my people. If she sees this, if she fears it and hates it as much as we do, then she is more likely to help us.

I know she's a kind person. I can see that from the moment I met her. She has a big heart, and she's been hurt before, but I know she's the Chosen One for a reason. The others, the fake ones and the useless ones, they were *never* the real chosen ones, not ever. Bella. It was always Bella, and the ones who came before her. Her ancestors.

I see that now. And all the suffering we've been through, all the nightmares and the hell I've lived through, will be worth it because of her.

"Welcome back, Bella," I whisper as I step around the rock where she last saw me. "I've been expecting you."

"Who are you? And what do you want from me?" Her voice is like music to my ears, even as she shouts at me, because at least her attention is directed at *me*.

"You're the Chosen One, the one our leader has prophesied would come and finally save us, finally set us free. You are the only one who can help us." My heart aches as she turns away from me. I don't blame her for being scared, and why would I? Even though I can't stand how I look and what I am now, I can't stop. I can't let her turn away from me again.

"I can't help you! I can't! I can't even help myself. Please, whoever you are, leave me alone! Leave me alone! Leave me alone!" Her voice tears at my heart, and all I want to do is reach out to her and hold her close.

I know this is terrifying, and I know I'm asking a lot from her, but she's our only hope, *my* only hope. I'm thrown back into reality again, left trembling and panting as I stare at her through her window, wishing that she would stop pushing me away. Every time, I get a little closer, but it's taking too long, and her rejections are like a knife to the heart, a knife twisting each time I'm thrown from her dreams.

I gasp for breath, a clawed hand pressed to my heaving chest as I force myself to breath, my heart thundering against my palm. I wonder if a heart can escape a person's body from beating too fast, because if it could, mine's about to. I watch her as she reaches for her phone, and I know she's calling him again. The beat of my heart slows as the icy tendrils of hatred creep into the back of my mind. I can't hear his voice, but I know he's there, regardless. I never realized I could hate someone more than I hate Asmodeus, or Lucifer, or even myself for my failings. But him? My resentment toward him is more than anything I can describe.

Scowling, I hook a claw under her window and open it before I even think about what I'm actually doing. I slip into her room and slink into the shadows, breathing heavily as I watch her on her bed. She's so close to me now, and I realize the significance of where I'm standing.

She's not getting away from me, not this time. I don't care that he has her heart. If she gives me the chance, I know I can show her how much more of a man I am than this pathetic *boy* of hers. As soon as she hangs up, I can't help but smile. I swear, she's going to hear me this time, and this time, she won't have a choice.

"Hello, Bella."

"Whoa!" she cries out, almost falling off her bed as she hears me speak.

I'm no longer a dream; I'm a reality. Her flashlight doesn't find me at first, and I know it's because her mind won't *let* me be real to her. That's why the other humans don't "see" me, not really, because they no longer believe in demons.

At least, the humans I've met so far don't, though I'm sure there are still plenty in this godforsaken town who believes in us, and it's them I have to avoid.

After a second, she stops and throws her hands over her mouth in fear. There. There it is; she can finally see me.

"Please, leave me alone," she whispers, hiding beneath her blanket as though, somehow, that's enough of a defense against something of my magnitude. She closes her eyes, and I move from my spot by the wall, closing the distance between us.

I reach out and grab her wrist, pulling her toward me. I can't wait any longer. I need her to stop hiding from me. She kicks me away, and for the moment, I let her, fading back into the half-reality of existence that I've been in with her for a little while. But that's okay. I'm getting closer now. She can't hide from me anymore, not really, not again.

I'm in her head.

CHAPTER 5

I'd touched her. Not just in a dream, where my imagination can run rampant, but something real. It's more than I ever believed was possible. All this time, all those millennia where I never felt anything for anyone. It wasn't something that was important to me, getting my family free from their nightmare was and still is, because it was my fault that they're trapped in this horror in the first place.

I stare at my hand, tracing my palm with my finger.

I didn't mean to fall in love with her. I know that my family was meant to be here with me so that we could take back what's rightfully ours, but I can't help how I feel.

She's seen me now. She's felt my hand on her arm, and I've left a mark. I never meant to hurt her, but part of me is also happy about it as well. My handprint is on her arm, marking her forever, reminding her that I'm always with her. Things are real for her now, and I need to keep it real so that she cannot keep pushing me away.

I hate that I'm going to have to hurt her first, but I promise I'll make it up to her, that I'll make everything right again. She wants to deny what she's seen, and something deep inside me understands that. Why would anyone want something like me to be real? But I need to be real to her, so that I can save my family once and for all.

This time, I won't leave. This time, I'm going to stay close to her. I'm going to drive her mad, make her angry, and force her to face me, just as I used my anger toward that dumb boy of hers to become real. She can only deny me for a little while. The more I subject her to my presence, unwanted or otherwise, the more likely it is that she will confront me, and then we can finally *talk*. I need her to listen to me so that I can get her help.

My body aches from the force of my intention coming into her reality the way it did, and part of me desperately wants to slink back into my cave and sleep, but I can't bear to leave Bella now. At the back of my mind, I'm aware that I'm following her around like some uninvited shadow, especially into private places like when she's bathing.

Of course, I'm curious. How can I not be? I'm dying to see her naked, to touch her, and make her moan in pleasure. I've never been with a woman like her, and I can barely contain my need for her.

She looks in the mirror as she dries her face with a towel, and she *sees* me. I smile, as softly as I can. I don't want to admit how glad I am when she jumps and screams. I know I shouldn't be. It's not the ideal reaction to her seeing my face, but it means she cannot ignore me now. She can push me away all she likes, but I'm a part of her world now, and I'm not going anywhere.

Where Bella goes, I go. I can see her trying not to look for me in every reflection, keeping her head down as though staring at the floor rather than looking over her shoulder might make me go away. She has two shadows now, and there is no way I'm leaving her side unless I have to... or unless I really start to push too hard too fast.

She's meeting with *him* again; of course, she is. I hardly expected her to stop seeing him *just* because she's seen me, but it doesn't hurt any less when he kisses her and touches her in all the ways I want to.

"You look like you've seen a monster."

I can't help but grin fiendishly at the words that slip from his tongue, and I'm glad when Bella bites back with her own words. Good. He's not little Mister

Perfect, and she's going to realize how much better off she'd be with me. He has *no* idea how truthful his words are, but it doesn't matter; I'm going to make him eat them before long.

There's something satisfying at his faux pas, and I can't stop grinning as I slide into the back of the car, technically too big for it given my horns — but such things don't worry me too much.

Spotting my reflection in the car mirror frightens her, though I'm hardly surprised at this reaction. The car swerves, and I delight a little in the boy's loss of control, and the fact that he gets frustrated with Bella.

That's it. Push her away; show her that she can't count on you. I coax softly, willing him to show Bella how truly insensitive he can be. I was never concerned about the car. *Had* the idiot lost control, I would have saved Bella myself. Of course, I would.

I watch carefully as the boy sighs at Bella, clearly not believing her as he climbs back into the car and starts driving again. It's hard not to laugh at him, to know that soon enough, I'm going to take her from him. Leaning forward, I gently run my black nails through her hair, sighing softly as I enjoy the feeling, until she pulls away from me.

I'm a little surprised at my own confidence. I've never been this bold, relying on my father and mother for strength, but I want her. The more I think about being with her, the harder it is to resist pushing her to her limit so that she will reach out to me. She stares at me, and all I can do is grin.

Soon. Soon, she'll be mine.

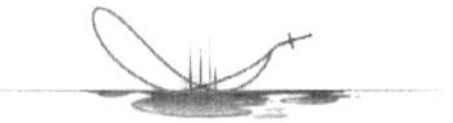

I DRAG my feet behind me, forcing myself to move my legs one in front of the other as I slump toward my cave. Try as I might, I cannot ignore the exhaustion that's seeping into my bones. Everything aches. The strain from forcing myself into Bella's reality, for *making* her see me and accept that I exist, has taken a toll on me, not to mention the fact that I barely slept the day before as it is.

I can see her paranoia growing every time she catches sight of me in the reflections of the glass on the classroom doors, or on the well-polished school floors. Every flinch, every whimper, every tear is another dagger in my heart because this is all *my* doing, but I need to make sure she doesn't forget me.

The moment she decides I'm not real is the moment I'm done for. I can haunt her dreams as much as I like, but she will convince herself that I don't exist, and then I won't be able to plead my case for my family. What good will I be to them then? If I can't get the Chosen One on my side, they will never be free.

I promise you, Bella. Once you understand, I'll make it right. I think to myself, clinging to that ray of hope.

Stumbling down the road, I grunt as I collide with something.

Panic hits me like a ton of bricks, and all the fatigue I'd been feeling vanishes in a second as the fear of discovery replaces it. My skin prickles, and my heart feels as though it's beating on a knife's edge as I hold my breath, waiting for whoever I'd bumped into to recognize what I am and finally turn against me. All because I'm too tired to keep my eyes open and stay alert.

"Uhm, sorry," the something says in a bleary tone.

Raising a brow, I blink at the man who's spoken and cannot help but smile. My fear washes away instantly, replaced by relief and a sense that I cannot *believe* my good luck. The second my blurry vision clears, I see who it is. Bella's older brother, Ash.

"Not a problem," I reply, smiling slightly.

"Hey, I don't suppose you know a good place to have a quick...," Ash makes a sign with his fingers and lifts his hand to his lips in a manner I don't understand, "somewhere private?" he asks.

"I guess? I know a place. If you don't mind walking a bit," I reply back.

In the back of my mind, I ask myself if it's wise, inviting this human back to the place that's become my sanctuary, but at the same time, I wonder if this might be just the opportunity I need to get into Bella's life elsewhere, to get to know her better. Honestly, at this point, anything can help.

"Hey, dude, as long as I can smoke without my

parents on my back, I don't care." Ash snorts. "You new here, too?" he asks.

"Err, yeah," I answer him, eyeing Ash carefully as I lead the way toward the outskirts of town and along the canal toward my mountain cave.

"Nice. You know, it's not that bad here. Most people just mind their own business, ya know? I'm just sick to death of this incessant rain!" Ash continues, his voice dreamy and content.

I can't believe how calm he is around me, like the man in the pub who keeps feeding me for free. Whatever he needs to smoke has clearly blinded him to my true form. That, or he just doesn't care. One or the other.

"I'm Ash, by the way. Ash Nova," he introduces himself, offering me his hand to shake. "Nice to make your acquaintance." He says it in such a posh tone, giggling and snorting in amusement at himself.

I can't help but grin in return, laughing softly as I take his hand and shake it. "Draven Asmodeus. Nice to meet you. Are you Bella Nova's brother?" I dare to ask.

"Ah, are you the one dating my sister?" he asks, eyes narrowing at me.

"No, that's someone else," I reply, unable to keep the hint of sadness from my voice.

"Oh, but you'd like to." Ash grins, handing over the small rolled up wad in his hand that's giving off the most disgusting smell.

"Yeah, you could say that." I laugh, taking the thing from him and following what he had been doing, lifting it to my lips and inhaling it. I cough, and Ash laughs.

"First timer?"

"Yeah." I cough, banging my fist on my chest.

"You'll get used to it." He chuckles, taking it back from me and taking a deep inhale on it. "Stick with me, kid. I'll teach you all that I know." He grins, patting me on my shoulder.

I grin back. I think I'm going to like being friends with Ash.

CHAPTER 6

Spending the day with Ash was exactly what I needed, and I know I have an ally here at the very least. Something about that bolsters me, knowing that I'm not fully alone anymore, that there's someone here I can turn to. I knew I'd been feeling lonely, but I hadn't realized just how heavy the weight of that had been until now.

Smoking whatever he had given me helped me sleep better than I have in what feels like ages. My mind feels free, and my heart is beating so slowly that I keep having to check that it hasn't stopped entirely as I escort Ash back to his house. He's more out of it than I am, so I didn't trust him not to walk out in front of one of those moving contraptions, or drown himself in the canal.

I wave goodbye to him and watch him go into the building before sneaking back into Bella's room, disappointed to find it empty for the first time since I've been contacting her.

Regardless, I slip into the room and lie down on her bed. Breathing it in slowly, relishing in the scent of her and moaning as I imagine her next to me. Closing my eyes, I focus all of my energy on her.

"Bella, Bella Nova." I call to her in her dream, strong and powerful as I drag her back to me.

I stand before her, exposed and alone, my eyes pleading as I look at her while she begs me to leave her alone. I can't. I mustn't. For the sake of my family, I *need* her.

"Bella, please, listen to me. I need your help. My family needs your help!" I plead, reaching out to her, only for her to be dragged into the waking world again. I won't leave, not this time. I'm not leaving until she listens to me.

I stay in her room, hiding in the shadows and out of the corner of her eye, but always close enough as she dresses up for *him*. I hate it. I want to go downstairs and rip his throat open with my nails, but I know I have to wait. I have to make her see. I watch out of her window as they drive away, feeling my heart ache as she vanishes from sight with him once again.

Draven! Please, we need you. They're killing us, Draven!

I wince and shake my head as my sister's panicked dream voice wiggles its way back into my mind. I haven't spoken to my family in days, not daring to reach out to them and admit that I still haven't been able to get Bella on my side, to admit that I'm still struggling to get her to *see* me. My mother would be understanding, but I can already hear the panic in her voice without even speaking to her.

The fear that I will fail, that I won't be able to free them as I had promised. It's not just her fear. It's my own, and as I sit in Bella's room surrounded by the darkness, I wonder if I was ever strong enough for this task.

Why couldn't it have been my sister? She might still be unable to fully control her powers, but she has more strength than *any* of us, and her own brand of chaos might just have been what we needed for this mission.

Asmodeus will kill me if I fail, if the humans don't, anyway. I know that I've been lucky so far, not to be caught by any of them who *might* know what I am. My biggest worry is that he will hurt my mother and sister because he cannot hurt me. I know the demons born in Hell are far more dangerous, and they all want to be free from the Underworld even more than my own people do. I want to be the one to free all of them, to show them that I'm much stronger than they thought I was.

No! I'm letting the despair take over again, letting my paranoia and fear rule me. I've come this far. I can, and I *will*, get Bella to see me for me. I know it. And I'm going to make her help us!

Just as I fix my resolve, I hear the door to the house slam, and footsteps race upstairs. For a moment, I wonder if it's Ash coming back home for another smoke, but I think he's now using my cave as his base for that. I know the parents are out, which just leaves...

"Bella." Her name flickers off my tongue before I even think about it, and I pull myself to my full height, one hand on the wall of her bedroom as though I can reach out and comfort the tears from here. Each sob wrenching at my heart as I want to tear apart the ones who have hurt her like this.

I watch quietly as she comes back into her room, climbing into her bed and turning off the infernal device for once, the boy's name finally cut off as she does so. So, he's finally hurt her enough, hasn't he? I hate that she's had to be betrayed for me to finally find my way into her heart, but I can't wait anymore. I *need* her.

"Bella Nova, save me," I whisper, stepping out of the darkness toward her.

She whimpers in return, pulling her blanket over her head and sobbing. "Please, not you."

"Bella. I'm sorry. I truly am, but I cannot afford to waste any more time. I need you." I add softly, kneeling on the floor beside her bed. "Not just my family, but me. *I* need you." There's a soft growl in my voice to reiterate my need, and I hate it. I don't want to frighten her in any way.

"Just leave me alone! I can't help you. I can't even help myself. Every time I let people in, I just get hurt, and I... I can't do it anymore!"

"Did he hurt you?" I growl, resting a hand on the edge of her bed, my nails digging into the mattress as my skin prickles with electricity, and my heart swells with anger. The thought of that human doing anything to upset Bella angers me.

"I... I... no."

I sigh heavily, getting up off the floor so that I can sit at the edge of her bed. I see her pull down her blanket a little so that she can stare at me, her eyes wandering over my body. I can see her fear melt away a little at the sight of my muscles, and I smile softly at her.

"I'm sorry. My appearance can be... frightening," I say softly.

"It... you're fine. Who are you?"

"I told you. My name is Draven Asmodeus, and I need your help."

"You said you needed help for you and your family?"

"That's right, but right now, that doesn't matter. All that matters to me is *you*." I smile at her.

"Why me? Why won't you just leave me alone?"

"Because you're special, Bella, in more ways than I

can count. I was sent here by my family because you're the only one who can help us, but I never expected to..."

"To what?" Bella asks, sitting up and staring at me closely, clearly intrigued.

"To fall for you," I admit, smiling again as I see her blush and look away.

"Flattery isn't going to make me want to help you more," she mutters.

I laugh and shake my head. "I mean it. From the moment I saw you, down by the canal, out in the rain alone."

"You've been following me since then?!" she snaps.

I flinch and look away. "You couldn't see me... because you weren't ready to. It seems that humans have forgotten about us and can't really see me for what I am."

"A demon?"

I nod and rub my face with my hands, my shoulders shaking as I both laugh and cry as she utters the word. I know what I am. I know what I've become, but that doesn't make it any easier to hear when coming from her. I don't want her to see me like this, but what choice do I really have? Without her, I will never be able to go back to who I was, and *this* is all I will ever be.

"Yes. You couldn't see me, either. Not at first; not until I used your dreams. And I'm sorry for that. I know I hurt you, and I know I made you feel like you were going insane, but I had to make you see me so we could talk. That, and... well, I wanted you to see *me*, like I can see you." I reach over and brush a strand of hair back from her face. I know it's a bold move, but at this point, what do I really have to lose?

She doesn't flinch or back away from me. In fact, she closes her eyes and leans into my simple movement, and I smile in return, grateful that she isn't entirely terrified of me. I can see that she's frightened, but that's more due to the unknown rather than *me*.

"I know you've heard it a hundred times before, Bella, and I know you don't know me, but I've watched you from the moment I escaped from my nightmare, and I've been captivated by you ever since. I know you, better than you know yourself, because I've been able to live in your dreams and see what even *you* don't want to admit to."

"Do you have any idea how much of an invasion of my privacy that is?!" Bella cries, throwing the covers from herself and stumbling from the bed and into the middle of the room, her eyes watering as tears begin to run down her cheeks. "Like, it's bad enough that I can't trust the people I *thought* loved me, and now you're telling me you've been stalking me *and* forcing yourself into my dreams without my permission?!"

"Bella, I know, and I'm sorry. I really am, but I don't have the luxury of being nice about all of this," I reply, getting up and following her across the room, my hands on her shoulders as I look down at her. "My family doesn't have that much time, not when they'll be forced to wait *another* thousand years before we can even *think* about stepping foot onto the surface of this Earth. When I was sent to find the Chosen One, I never imagined she'd be this beautiful girl who I'd fall in love with."

Bella gasps at my words, and I flinch. It's all coming out wrong, but I have to make her understand. "You love me?" she mutters, reaching out to touch my arm, her fingers like a flame on my skin.

I jump at her touch, the place where her fingers linger on my skin tingling as though I've been electrified. For the first time in five millennia, I feel like I'm alive, and I can't help but become aroused, thinking about how it would feel to have her hands explore the rest of my body.

I should be ashamed of myself. I know I should, but I'm lost in how I feel about her. My heart swells painfully whenever I think of Bella, and being able to talk to her now?

Without thinking, I grab her wrist and pull her into my embrace, holding her close to me. My breath catches in my throat, and I growl gently, nothing like the sound a predator might make when hunting its prey. It's softer, more sexual, hungry as though I'm struggling not to devour her. I want to, not for food, but I want to taste her.

"Oh!" She giggles, and I blush.

"I-I'm sorry." I move to step away, realizing that she can probably feel me against her, but her fingers grasp at my shirt, and she holds me close. "Bella...," I whisper.

"How do I know I can trust you? Daven said he loves me, said I could trust him, and then..."

"Whatever happened, Bella, do you honestly believe that he didn't know what was going on? I heard you come back crying. I don't know what went on, but I know this. If you had been *my* girl, and I'd seen you upset, then *nothing* in this world would have stopped me from chasing after you. Or banging down the door in order to find you and make it all better. If he truly wanted to make you believe he knew nothing, why is he not here?" I ask.

It was a genuine question. I really didn't understand why he hadn't come to her home if he *truly* loves her the way I love her. I gasp as Bella's fingers trace my stomach, as if reassuring herself that I'm actually real.

"I know you don't really know me, Bella, but I have *never* lied to you. Not once, and I never will. I know my methods have been a bit... rough, but I didn't know how else to approach you, and without you being able to see me in reality, I had no hope of contacting you. And you're our only hope, *my* only hope, not just to save my family, but to save me," I whisper, desperate for her to accept me for who I am and see that I mean everything I'm saying to her. "I will never lie to you, Bella. I mean that. You see me as I am now, at my worst, and if you stay with me, I will prove to you that I mean it. That I'm being truly honest with you."

Her fingers brush against my cheek, and I look down into her eyes, those deep green pools that I could stare into for *hours* without ever getting bored. I want her more than I can ever explain, but how do I show her?

"Do you want me?" she asks, shocking me.

"Yes, I thought that was *somewhat* obvious," I reply, a bit confused. "But I don't want to rush you, either. I know all about your dreams, remember? I know your life because of your nightmares, because of your innermost thoughts, and I... I don't want to push you into something that you're not ready for. No matter *how much* I want you, and how often I've dreamt about you." I growl.

She presses her body against mine, and I hold her close, lifting her chin gently with a finger as I lean down to her. I can feel her breath upon my skin, and I shiver in anticipation, my nerves on fire as I finally relent and press my lips to hers. She tastes even sweeter than I had imagined, but kissing her only makes me want her more, if that's even possible.

Breaking the kiss, I gasp for breath, my hands trembling on Bella's back as I keep her close. "I'm sorry. I just couldn't help myself."

"It's fine, really. I actually enjoyed it." She smiles back at me, her hand resting on my chest and over my racing heart. "I think I need this as much as you do."

A sharp pain stabs me in my heart, and part of me wonders if she's only using me to get back at *him* for upsetting her, but another part of me wonders if I should even care if that's why she wants me. All I've wanted since I first saw her is to hold her like this, to show her how *I* can make her feel good.

Growling low in my throat, I pick her up in my muscular arms and gently carry her to her bed. I hear the sharp inhale of breath, the shock at my strength evident, but she's still not afraid of me. I lay her down and smile at her as she wraps her legs around my waist, making my heart leap into my throat. This girl will be the death of me, in the best way possible.

I slide one hand under her garment, sighing happily as she groans with pleasure as my fingers caress her naked breast, my free hand tracing a line up her inner thigh.

My wildest dreams can't remotely compare to the reality of her breathy moans down my ear, and there's no way I can deny how hard she makes me, not when I'm pressing against her wet bottoms as I lie on top of her. I bury my face into her neck and breathe her in. If this is the only chance I get to be with her, then I'm going to savor every luscious second of it.

I feel her weight shift beneath me, her hands clawing at my back as I touch her through her bottoms, unable to stop myself, whimpering as I feel how wet she is, but I'm still conscious of not wanting to push her too far too fast.

"Are you sure?" I growl softly, looking down into her eyes, my heart hers for the rest of my long existence. "Because once I take you, I'm not sure I'll be able to stop myself."

"I'm sure; make me yours," she whispers, but it's hard to ignore the tears in her eyes.

Removing my hand from her garment, I wipe the

tears from Bella's cheeks with my thumb and smile at her. "No man should ever make you cry, Bella. Never. No man is ever worth your tears."

I want her, but I want to prove to her that I'm not him. If I'm ever going to have her heart, then I need her to see that I'm different from the others, from all those boys who *just* want to be inside her for their own pleasurable needs and gains rather than for Bella's.

I roll off her and see the look of shock on her face, mingling with rejection. I can imagine that it's not often a man has ever stopped halfway through sex with her, but I'm not going to be like any of them; I want her for her. Lying next to her, I pull Bella against me, pressing her head gently against my chest so she can hear my racing heartbeat.

"It's okay. I can wait. I've waited five millennia for you. What's a day, a week, a month?" I smile down at her and kiss her head gently.

"You mean that... don't you?" she mutters into my chest, her tears soaking my body as she clings to me tightly.

"I do. As much as I want you, I don't want to push you into it. I know you're thinking about him. I don't want my first time to be about him and not me."

"Your first time?!" Bella gasps, pushing me away gently to stare at me incredulously. "You mean..."

If my ashen black skin could blush, I would have been bright red at what I'd just stupidly admitted to, but I promised Bella that I'd be honest with her, and that's the reality of it. I never took a woman before our banishment; we were far more religious about such things when I'd been human. There were tussles in the hay, little touches here and there, but most of us didn't have sex for the fear of getting pregnant before marriage. We'd never have lived it down, been outcasts in our homes because of it, so it only happened on rare occasions... or for me, not at all.

"I've never been with anyone before. Ever. You would be my first, but I want you to be mine when *you* want to be mine. Not out of anger at someone else."

"Daven," she utters his name as though she just remembered that he exists. "I should call him back." She reaches over and grabs her phone, clutching it to her chest as her thumb hangs over one of the buttons, clearly debating whether or not to call him like she had just said.

Her words are like a knife to my heart. I've bared my soul to her, been honest and restrained myself, as difficult as that has been given how all I want is to feel her wrapped around me.

"Can you trust what he'll say if you do?" I ask, unable to keep my contempt for him from my voice.

She turns and smiles, snorting at my obvious jealousy. "No. Not really... I know he'll tell me that he didn't know anything about it, that he had nothing to do with it, but how can I trust if he's going to tell me the truth? When I told him I was seeing you, he took me to a doctor. He clearly thinks I'm as crazy and insane as those bitches at school think I am. Otherwise, why would he have left me alone *just* as they targeted me with that... box of stuff." She scowls at the phone and tosses it to one side, curling back into my arms. "You're right... I can't trust him. I can't trust any of them. You're the only one who has ever been truly honest with me." Then she takes a deep breath and sighs. "Draven?"

"Yes, Bella?"

"Will you stay here with me tonight?" she asks so quietly that I almost don't hear her.

"Bella, I would like nothing more than that." I smile, kissing her forehead and breathing her in as I pull her closer.

The sound of her breathing grows softer as she drifts to sleep, and it soothes me. And it's also hard to fight my own exhaustion. The day has been a roller coaster, but in that moment, I'm content with the woman of my dreams wrapped up in my arms.

CHAPTER 7

"Bella! Bella, darling, are you up yet?" Her mother's voice calls up to us, waking us both up with a jolt.

"Oh my god! Can you hide?" Bella hisses.

"Not easily, though chances are, she may ignore me entirely. Though, she may see me as a weird-looking human... I can go out the window?" I grin.

"No, I'm not having you crawl out my window. Just... stay here a minute. Let me get rid of her. I still have some questions I want to ask you. If that's okay?" she asks, putting a brush through her hair after she pulls on the same garment from last night.

"You can ask me whatever you want. I'll wait here, and if it looks like someone's coming in, I'll go out the window, but not until I'm sure someone who isn't you is coming in." I smile.

"Thank you," Bella whispers, throwing her arms around me and standing on her toes to kiss me.

"Bella?" her mother calls again.

"I'm up!" Bella snaps back.

"Oh, good. Daven's here. He wants to see you."

Bella freezes, her hand on the handle of her bedroom door at the mention of his name. She begins to tremble, her fingers white as she grips the handle tightly.

I hate him. I hate him for ever having the chance to hurt her the way he has, just like all the other men in her life. None of them have deserved her. Not one of them.

"Bella. Go see him if you need to. I can wait here for you or come back later," I whisper to her, placing a hand on her shoulder to reassure her.

"No. I want you to stay. I want *you*, not him," she says angrily, turning her head to kiss my fingers before turning back to the door. "I don't want to see him, Mom. Tell him to go away!"

"Oh... okay. I'm sorry, Daven. She says she doesn't want to see you." Her mother's muffled voice drifts up to us as Bella stands by the door, listening in.

"Bella? Bella, please! Just let me talk to you; let me explain!" Daven calls up to her.

"No! I don't want to hear what you have to say. Just go and see your slut, Stephanie, and leave me alone!" Bella snaps, throwing herself into my arms and hugging me tightly.

I pull her close, unable to keep myself from grinning as she chooses me over that buffoon. Her breathing is labored as her hands cling to my back. Her body presses close to mine, her breasts a hard lump against my body.

"Bella...," I warn her gently, feeling the sudden arousal against my bottoms.

"I want you. I want *you*. I want someone who isn't going to lie to me, who's going to respect me. I want someone who *sees* me." She snarls, her fingers running along my stomach and making me moan in anticipation, desperate for more. "*You* see me. You've always seen me, haven't you? From the minute you found me sitting in the rain by the canal, sneaking your way into my dreams and seeing the worst parts of my life... yet you're still here, and you still love me. I want you. I want *you*, Draven."

It's all I need to hear, and it's the permission I required to let myself go. The growl that leaves my throat frightens me with its lust-filled ferocity as I pin her against the wall, my hand holding her wrists above her head as I nibble at her neck. I had promised to make her mine, and now she's going to be.

She writhes and moans at my touch, wiggling to

free herself so that she can touch me in return. Freeing her, we hurriedly take off each other's clothes, and I groan at the sight of her. She's even more beautiful than I could ever have imagined.

The bed is forgotten. I hold her up against the wall and slide inside her with a whimper, feeling her hot and wet parts against me. If I were ever to touch Heaven, this is it, here with Bella in my arms, lost in this sensational pleasure.

When we finish, we collapse onto her bed in each other's arms, panting heavily. I run my finger along her wrist, my eyes drawn to the handprint, *my* handprint, on her arm. "I'm sorry. I never realized I would mark you when I grabbed you."

"It's alright; it doesn't hurt. I suppose I'm marked as yours, better than a ring." Bella laughs. "It's clearly fate. That reminds me, you keep saying that I'm the Chosen One, and that I'm the only one who can help save your family. What do you mean?" she asks, shifting around so she can sit on my lap, wrapping her legs around my back, and making me shudder as her naked breasts brush against my chest.

"You keep that up, and I'm going to be unable to answer." I growl teasingly, running my fingers through her hair. "My family and I, we weren't always demons. Once, we were humans, natives to this land who lived peacefully amongst the other humans who also lived here. Only, the peace didn't last."

I sigh heavily, leaning back against her wall as I ready myself to tell the story of my life. I've never uttered the words aloud to anyone before; it was always my father who reached out to coax the Chosen One onto our side... until he died, and the role fell onto my shoulders instead.

"My family, my tribe, we were deemed evil by some of the other humans. Though I think it was just jealousy and greed. They wanted our land, but we wouldn't give it up, so they called us evil and said we didn't belong. I was young and reckless, and I was sick of my people being bullied and butchered by the other natives, so I stood up to them. The problem was, I stood up to the wrong person."

"What do you mean?" Bella asks, scowling at me.

"I decided to go after one of the other humans who was against us. I stole her livestock and destroyed her crops, like they had done to us, and I mouthed off at her. What I *didn't* know was that the woman I'd targeted was a witch. Because I was young and reckless, I doomed my family, my entire tribe of people, my entire generation, into the abyss of Hell." I croak as the words force themselves from the back of my throat. I know what I'd done was wrong, but I'd never been given the chance to redeem myself.

"She cast us into the abyss, doomed to live in the Underworld with the demons. Some of my people got eaten the minute we arrived. Others, like myself, got turned into demons as well. But we still lived in fear of the others, that they might turn against us at any minute and kill us like the others. Our human souls were trapped in an amulet of yellow and purple, which is why this whole fucking town wears those colors; it helps to keep the spell intact, keep it strong."

"But you got out? How?" she asks.

"Every thousand years, we get the chance to come to the surface. It's said that the Chosen One is the *only* one who can help us be free again. I know it's a lot to ask. I know it's a lot to put on you, but without you, my family is stuck in that pit of fire for another thousand years, in that searing void until the next time the surface opens again, and we can be set free. The portal closed early this time. I was meant to come through with my family, but I was the only one who got out."

"You're alone...," Bella whispers, her hand on my cheek.

"I am, and without you, I'll always be alone. Without you, Bella, I'll never die. I'll never free my family from the Underworld, and I'll never be human again. All because I made a mistake when I was younger."

"And they never gave you a chance to say you're sorry?" Bella asks, her tone growing angry, not at me, but at those who had thrown me into Hell in the first place.

"No. I've had a long time to reflect on my actions. I could have lived with *myself* being thrown into the abyss as punishment, but my family never deserved any of this. None of us deserved the curse that the witch put on us. They started the war against us. All I did was stand up for my people, and they cast us into Hell."

I can see Bella thinking it all over, and I wonder what she thinks about it. I'd had millennia to be angry, to hate humans, to want to see them suffer as we suffered, but this is all still new to her. I'm putting a lot of pressure on her, since my entire tribe is relying on her help to break the curse.

"You didn't do anything wrong, though. None of you. How could they act like you're evil when they were the ones pressuring you in the first place? This was your home, and they took it from you!" she yells angrily.

I nod. I hadn't realized how comforting it would be to tell someone our story, to hear someone agree that our punishment didn't fit our crime, even my own.

"And this entire town is in on it! All of them!" Bella snaps, her hands balled into fists. "Draven, I'll help you. I'll do whatever it takes to free your family and get your human souls back. None of you deserves this. I bet Daven knows all about this as well... I thought I could trust him, but he and his family have all made sure that none of you could live the lives you should have. I promise you, Draven. Whatever I can do to help, I will," she says firmly, placing her hands on my face and staring into my eyes.

I smile at her, hugging her tightly and kissing her hard. "Bella, thank you so much. I love you, and my family is in your debt." I gasp, kissing her again, smiling as she kisses me back.

Mom, Melanesia. You'll be free soon. The Chosen One is on our side now. You're coming home.

UNLEASHING HELL BOOK TWO

LOVING HER

VIOLA TEMPEST

UNLEASHING HELL BOOK THREE

SAVING THEM

VIOLA TEMPEST

CHAPTER 1

BELLA NOVA'S POV

The clock on the wall is the loudest thing I have ever heard, and I'm counting the ticks like the gun that had gone off when I killed Brick.

Tick. Tock. Tick. Tock.

Dr. Schultz is waiting for me to say something, but I don't know where to start. I'm wearing an oversized sweater to cover up the mark that he'd left. I still don't know what had come over me. I like to think I'm not one to ask based on emotion. I like to think that I can do an okay job of thinking about consequences, considering the logic of things. But my track record isn't looking great.

Schultz taps his pen against his notebook, waiting.

Draven? I whisper it into my brain. I try it on the left side; I try it on the right. I try it in the front, and I try it in the back. I try to say his name through my body, sending it down to my toes. It's impossible to know when he's around. But I think I've figured out his kryptonite.

"I'm worried," I finally say between the tapping of the pen and the ticking of the clock. I can't focus, can't search my body for him until I *can* focus.

The pen clicking stops.

Draven?

"Be more specific. About whom, dear? About what? When did it start?"

I noticed it a day or two ago. The kryptonite, not the worry. It made as much sense as something could when you're grasping at straws. Draven gets weaker—loses his hold on me—when I think of sunshine. He's a demon, so maybe it all adds up.

However, thinking of sunshine isn't enough when someone is already inside your head. It feels like whenever I begin to contemplate the warmth of a summer day, imagine the blinding light that one might see from staring straight into the sun, he's slamming down a brick wall. Now I *am* the sunshine. I have, discreetly, rubbed my arms and the back of my neck with the essence of lemon.

My sweater is yellow. I'm wearing a sun ring on the finger next to my pentagram ring, another one of the many pieces of jewelry mother had given me from her odd collection.

For now, I think Draven is at bay.

"About me," I finally say. Schultz raises an eyebrow but doesn't say anything else. He wants me to explain. "I've been... feeling unlike myself."

He shifts in his seat. "Tell me more."

"Well," I sigh, crossing one leg over the other, "I've been... making rash decisions. I've been distrustful, yet too trusting all at once. I'd say I'm paranoid, maybe. I've been... having these nightmares."

"You mentioned those last time." Schultz nods his head as if he already knows. He scribbles a few things down. "It may help if you give me specifics, Ms. Nova."

I take a deep breath. What instance can I tell him without making me seem insane? How can I sound just insane enough so that he gives me advice, a prescription, but doesn't admit me into a hospital?

Should I be going to a hospital?

I hate myself for thinking of Stephanie. I can't even figure out the right answer, think critically about whether or not I need to go stay somewhere for a while to get my mental health in order. Rumors would get around. And Stephanie will win.

"Like... with Daven," I try to explain. Schultz leans

forward, peers at me over his glasses, but doesn't add anything. "Is it okay if I talk about him?"

He lets out a slight professional chuckle as he sits back against his chair. "Why wouldn't it be?"

"Well, aren't his family members clients of yours? I don't want to offend—"

"I'm a doctor, Bella," he interrupts me, setting his notebook on the side table next to him. "I can't disclose to them anything you say. I have no favorites. They're a lovely family, but trust that anything you say is between you and I."

"Okay," I mumble, sitting up. "I guess I can give you an example. With Daven."

"Sure," he nods.

"We broke up." I feel a sadness in my chest, though I'm usually more angry than sad. "And... I don't know if it's my fault or not."

"Explore that. Talk about that more."

"Something happened." I scratch the back of my neck, hoping that breaking the surface of my skin will allow the essence of lemon to hide me from Draven. "With this girl at school. She hates me, and she embarrassed me, and I... could have communicated with him better about it. But I just... felt like everything was.... like it had all been a part of this big conspiracy to hurt me."

"The paranoia." Schultz nods, taking the notebook and scribbling again. "That's a common thing for many mental... dilemmas."

I notice him not trying to say ill. I don't care if he

says I'm mentally ill. I almost want him to—maybe that means I just need a bowl of chicken soup, a little rest, and a cold compress pressed to the front of my skull to freeze Draven out.

"Sure," I mumble again, shifting in my seat. "Sure. Yeah, maybe it was silly of me to think that Daven could have anything to do with what Stephanie did—"

"And what did she do?" He crosses one leg over his knee and peers over his glasses again. I take another deep breath. Does he feel like a dentist? Pulling teeth?

"At the homecoming dance—the one Daven took me to—she... ugh. It was awful! I don't even want to talk about it. She humiliated me in front of the whole school."

"And you think Daven helped?"

"No, of course not."

"So, why were you upset with him? Walk me through that thought process. Tell me what you were thinking when you decided you didn't want to communicate in the way that you—as you have mentioned—thought would be successful."

I shrug. "I guess there was a... voice in my head."

He perks his eyebrows up. "A voice—"

"Not a real one!" I jump in quickly, and we both smile. "Sorry, I'm new to therapy."

"Everyone is at one point. And that's okay. Tell me what you want to tell me, and I will respect your privacy. When I'm asking these questions, Bella," he smiles when says my name, refers to me as a friend, "it's to guide you to a different understanding of what you have already said. Yes?"

I shake my head yes and continue. "There was a little voice in my head, an itch, that said if Daven really cared about me, he would have chased after me. And made sure I was alright. This happened less than a week ago, and he's already dating someone new. And I know it's because *I* am already dating someone new, but—"

"Let's pause here." Dr. Schultz puts his pen and notepad back down on the coffee table, grabs his coffee mug, and leans forward before taking a sip. "You're already dating someone new? And this only happened a week ago?"

Draven? I whisper it again and hear nothing. But how am I supposed to know if he's just hiding somewhere, watching over me, waiting to hear what I say about him? I'm careful about my word choice. I don't want to know what might happen if Draven gets angry.

"He was there for me when Daven wasn't. He has this... energy. It's like a magnetic connection. I don't know how to explain it."

"Do you feel this way a lot?" he asks. I feel as though it's a trick question.

I quickly answer, "No!"

But maybe I do. Maybe I've felt these magnetic, fatal attractions to others for whatever reason. What about Brick? What about Daven? And Draven?

I'm looking down at my fingernails, picking at the acrylics I got for the homecoming dance. They're beginning to lose their shine, and there's a gap between the nail and my cuticle. Daven had paid for me to get them done.

When I look back up at Schultz, he's smirking. "It seems like you're thinking about your answer a little more critically now."

I deflate, leaning my head against the cushion of the old couch. The lighting in here is relaxing to some, I'm sure, but it isn't to me. He has lamps, not fluorescents. The lamps are on their lowest setting, making mostly everything cast an eerie shadow. *Draven?* But none of the shadows transform. I am relieved, and still suspicious, and still paranoid, all at once.

"I guess I do feel like I fall for people pretty fast."

He nods. "Do you think it's healthy for you to jump back into something so quickly after Daven?"

I shrug. "You're supposed to tell me."

"How was your relationship with Daven, Bella? Was it... safe?"

I scrunch my eyebrows, tilting my head back. "Safe? What do you mean?"

"Well, if I can be blunt," he explains, "it's pretty peculiar for a client to come to me about their significant other unless it's couples' counseling. Except for, of course, if the significant other is worried their partner will say something they shouldn't."

"What do you mean?"

"How'd you get that mark on your wrist, Bella?"

I look down. Just barely, the mark that Draven had left on me is peeking out.

"Oh," I pull down my sleeve self-consciously, "that wasn't Daven. Daven was nothing but respectful toward me."

"Okay," he sits back, "I just want to make sure this wasn't an... abusive situation. I was hoping he hadn't forced you into not telling me the whole truth."

"No, he would never do that."

"So, *is* that the whole truth?"

The clock is ticking so loudly. Shadows are shooting across the room as he moves, always forward and back, and forward and back, the shadow of his pen projecting across the wall. I feel highly anxious; I feel sweaty! What *is* the whole truth?

"I think I'm seeing things. And no one else seems to see them. Not... not *real* things. I'm just—paranoid, Dr. Schultz. And anxious. And I feel like there's two of me. Not that I have a split personality or anything like that—but there's a version of me that makes great decisions, plans things out, and then there's another version me that just takes these leaps that don't end up going right in the long run."

He nods. "This sounds like, at least from our first conversation, a case of Bipolar Disorder. I think you are manic when you're making these big, leaping decisions, Bella. And those with Bipolar Disorder—"

"I have Bipolar Disorder?" I repeat as a question. I try to think of what I know about Bipolar Disorder, and this just doesn't fit. "I'm not having mood swings, though."

"That's a common misconception," he explains. "Most people with Bipolar Disorder swing between mania and depression. The mania is sometimes glorious highs of making wild decisions—selling everything you own and moving to a convent, quitting your job without notice for no good reason, purchasing several instruments though you've never played. And then comes the depression. The loneliness, the exhaustion."

"Hm," I whisper. That's all I can say.

"Those who are bipolar may jump into relationships. They may have an intensity. And their intensity may become reflected by others, especially those who also have something going on."

"So, what's the cure?"

"No cures here," he said, scribbling. "You'll have to take medication, continue seeing me, and work at making adjustments. In time, it's a truly controllable disorder, especially in your case. It seems to be mild. Let's try you out on some mood stabilizers and see if they help. You can come back to see me in a week."

He's already handing me a script from his pad, with a funny name written across it in bad handwriting.

"But... what if I don't have Bipolar Disorder?"

"Then the pills probably won't help, but they won't hurt you, either. Let's go ahead and schedule our next appointment for next week." He moves from his armchair and goes over to his desk, looking through his calendar. "Same time? Same day?"

I look at the word again. I can't even make out all the letters, and I pray that a pharmacist will be able to.

"Would Bipolar Disorder give me hallucinations?" I ask. It sounds abrupt coming out of my mouth. I sound scared, though I don't mean to.

He whips his head around, face in a poorly disguised horror. "Bella, are you having hallucinations?"

I shake my head rapidly. "No. I was just asking. Same time, same day, next week."

I get up quickly, grabbing my purse, and I bolt out the door.

CHAPTER 2
BELLA NOVA'S POV

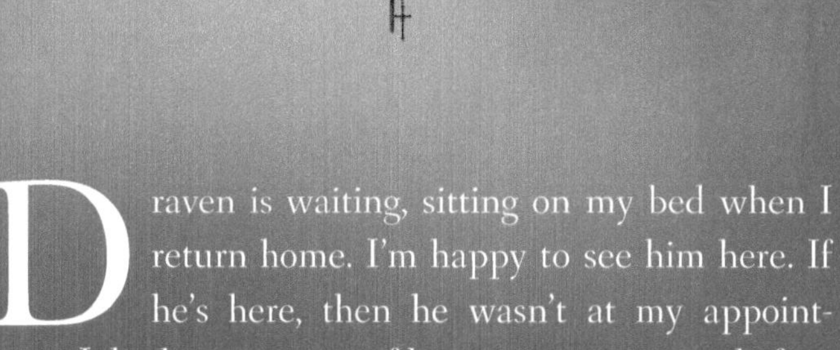

Draven is waiting, sitting on my bed when I return home. I'm happy to see him here. If he's here, then he wasn't at my appointment. I ditch my essence of lemon into my purse before hanging it up on the back of my door, sliding next to him on the bed. I slide my hand into his.

"How was the... dentist?" he asks. He doesn't understand what a dentist is, in the same way he doesn't understand what a street taco is or why one might purchase a car. I put the new bottle of pills I picked up at the pharmacy on my dresser.

"I have a cavity," I lie, leaning my head onto his shoulder.

"Is that what those are for?" he asks, nodding his head toward the pill bottle. "Those are very bright. Can you put them away?"

With this, I confirm my suspicions. He doesn't like yellow. He doesn't like orange. Anything that reminds me of sunshine makes him feel sick. Without speaking, I get up and grab my pills. I open up my sock drawer and put them at the bottom, covering them up with the socks. Dr. Schultz made it clear that I don't need my parents to consent to my treatment, and I'm not even sure how they'd feel about it.

I don't think of my parents as anti-mental health in general, but before I went to Schultz, I did a lot of self-reflection. I thought about PTSD, about my childhood, about my upbringing. Mom and dad were always great supporters and advocates for us—but had it been *us*? Or had it only been Ace, who was always getting into trouble at school and constantly smoking pot in his room?

Mom was always hovering, but she did it in the smartest way possible. She didn't tell me I couldn't do things or accuse me of this and that—instead, she weaseled her information through kindness. And once she figured out what she wanted to know, it seemed like the solution was a conversation between her and dad. But I wasn't in on those conversations.

Then, things mysteriously seemed to solve themselves.

Like in the third grade. I was in a class above my grade level because I was doing so well, and funding cuts had just taken the gifted and talented program away. There was a teacher's assistant, who was a high school or college associate or *something* to that extent, who had taken a special interest in me.

I don't even remember her name anymore, because things got shut down just like that. A snap of a finger. She had helped me research these folktales, had encouraged me to learn more about them, and I had let it slip to mom. Quite honestly, as interested and excited as I was about the stories, they were making it impossible for me to sleep. I was having horrific night-mares, I was losing my appetite, and I was getting these dark circles under my eyes. Mom found out and snapped. I never saw that girl again.

"You're looking more and more human by the minute," I tell Draven, giving him a once-over. He's wearing an old pair of Ace's jeans and one of his hood-ies. His nails, which used to be long and black, have been painted over with a neutral shade and clipped just enough to make him look more normal.

His skin has a healthy glow, thanks to my mother's foundation and my fathers "secret" concealer. He almost looks human if I avoid staring at him for too long. And no one else would. Something about his demon state makes him only half-visible at any given moment.

He's like something in your peripheral vision. When he isn't focused on you, you're not focused on him. He wouldn't jump or scare you if you did start to notice, either.

I wonder if it's an evolutionary tactic on our part. If one were to notice a demon and be frightened by it, it would just feed them more. It would just make the demon stronger. I've noticed the way my negative emotions exponentially grow when I'm around Draven: anger, fear, resentment, sadness, *guilt*. And I've noticed how he feeds on it.

"It seems like I'll need to look the part in order to save my family," he says. He is suspicious as he watches me from across the room. "I don't like your garment."

"Okay," I reply, simply taking it off and putting it in the laundry basket. Underneath, I'm wearing a black and purple tank top with stripes on it.

"I love that color!" he cheers, smiling mischievously.

"Black?" I laugh. "Not surprising."

He shakes his head. "The other one."

"Purple?"

"Purple. Yes, I know what it's called. I've just been going mad here. It's so different compared to where I'm from." He gets off the bed and closes the distance between us, putting his hands on my hips. I give him a soft smile but look away. "What is it?"

"I'm just tired, and my teeth hurt," I lie. I climb onto the bed and crawl under the top sheet, the one too small for him to fit under. *Regret*. Regret and guilt are exemplified through my bones right now, through my breathing. It feels like all I am is regret and guilt. I no longer feel human at all. I'm now closer to what Draven is; I know this for sure.

"What did they do to you, my sweet?"

I want to cringe at the word, but I don't.

"Can you go over the plan with me again?" I ask quietly.

"We will save my family," he says.

"But how? What do I have to do?"

He sighs, sitting on the edge of the bed. "Have I done something wrong, Bella?"

I feel a tear coming out of the corner of my eye. I try not to sniffle. The sadness is magnified now.

"How do I even know you're real?"

"Because I'm right here."

"That doesn't mean anything. The human brain can create hallucinations. It can create sounds and noises and feelings. This could all be a fucking hallucination. How *humiliating*. How freaky. I'm a freak!"

I say all of these things out loud, though I have spoken them in my head since the first time I met Draven. And it's true that Draven, since that day, has been nothing but kind to me. But this just gets weirder and weirder, and I think I've gone past the point of no return.

If I'd been honest about the hallucinations the first time around, would I be enjoying normal high-school girl things right now? Or would I still be here, on my bed, in an ever-flowing river of sadness and anger and fear, speaking to a demonic creature that may or may not even be real?

"You *want* to be crazy," he tells me. Getting off the bed, he goes to the corner and into my sock drawer. I don't even stop him. He moves my socks around until he finds the bottle.

"These aren't for your teeth; I'm willing to stake everything on it. I'm going to ask your brother."

He goes toward the door.

"Why would I *want* to be crazy?" I ask. He stops in his tracks and looks over his shoulder.

"Being crazy would be easier than believing in demons. It would be easier than accepting that you are the Chosen One, that many may die at your hands, and it'll be for a justice you refuse to understand."

He moves through the door stealthily, turning into a shadow as he crawls toward my brother's room. Ace is high, that I know for sure—it smells like a skunk in my bedroom because the window is open, and he likes to blow smoke out the window. What he doesn't know is that the wind usually blows it at me. I shake my head, getting up to light a candle, and lie back down.

My phone buzzes. It's Daven.

Can we talk?

I shake my head as though he can see me, and then I put my phone inside my bedside table drawer. I can hear it buzz a few more times, but I don't want to look. I don't care to look. Any chance of reconciliation that Daven and I had ended when he and Stephanie started dating. And you know what?

I open up my bedside table drawer again and grab both a pen and a sheet of paper. I write down, for Dr. Schultz, more thoughts. I don't want to forget all of this next week.

Why would Daven date Stephanie unless he was in on the prank? I write. *Maybe I'm not paranoid. Maybe I'm just gaslighting myself.*

I'm proud of myself for using the word "gaslighting," a word I'd found during my research. Bipolar Disorder hadn't come up a single time, but psychosis had. If I were in psychosis, wouldn't Ace be, too? He could see Draven. Most people could.

What worries me is that psychosis doesn't have to mean things just popping up out of the air as hallucinations. It could mean seeing something, something that was really real, and your mind twisting the image. It could distort it to have a brand-new meaning, to make their words sound different, to make your understanding of them different.

Kind of like when you dream, and you're at school with no shoes on, but so is everyone else, and your youth pastor is there. And your dog that died when you were seven is teaching the class, and it all just makes sense because your dream brain makes you *think* this is reality. What if that's what I'm doing with Draven? What if he's just some man who found me on the street, who's been stalking me, and now lives in my room?

Draven returns with the pill bottle.

"A mood stabilizer?" he asks. "To make your moods more... consistent?"

I nod. He hasn't gone into the muck of why I want to use them—because I'm crazy, and I'm scared.

"Yes," I mutter quietly, pulling the blanket up to my chin.

He sits on the bed, frowning. "Oh, Bella. I'm sorry. Demons tend to have this effect on people. No wonder you seem so sad."

"What effect?"

"Every negative emotion you've ever had in your life is going to be heightened around me. I thought that since you're the Chosen One, it would be different. But I was wrong. It sounds like it happens even *worse* for you. I'll turn it off."

"Turn it off?"

"Yes."

"You can just do that?"

"Sure," he says. "For you, I will. Just a matter of thinking about it."

I smile a little, hopeful that he's right, and my moods might stabilize on their own. But why then, has this happened to me my entire life, even before Draven? I push this thought out. Draven will solve this problem. Maybe it never existed before him. If I can be happy again, calm, I'll stop worrying about the past.

"I'm sorry for being so distant," I whisper to him. And I mean it.

I was all over Draven the day before. I was all over Draven the day before that. And I've been all over

Draven since we slept together. Today's swing in the other direction *must* have been prompted by his demonic traits, not by me. And he's not doing all this on purpose.

He crawls under the tiny blanket with me and gives me a kiss on top of my forehead, repeating the same sentiment that he's repeated to me a hundred times since we met.

"I've been waiting over five millennia to meet a girl like you, Bella Nova."

CHAPTER 3
DAVEN PORTER'S POV

My heart stops when I see Bella at school. Not in the way it usually does—usually when I see her, I feel my hands get a little clammy, and I can feel my forehead start to sweat. She's made me feel like a babbling idiot, not the calm and collected person I used to be around women.

Stephanie, though she does have beauty in her own way, doesn't make me nervous at all. Bella, the most beautiful girl I've ever seen in *her* own way, makes me buckle at the knees.

But today, when I see her, it's not her beauty or my regret or my promise (the promise I haven't promised her yet for the fear that it will compromise this mission: *I PROMISE I will not let Stephanie get away with this*) that shakes me. It's the boy she's holding hands with.

There's something off about him. Not just that he's holding hands with my beloved. I'll admit that I *am* jealous of him, and that may be skewing my perception. But it feels as though he walks around with this aura of superiority, maturity, and understanding of the world that guys my age just don't really have.

He's here, at the high school, and he's wearing jeans and a hoodie. His face looks smooth, wrinkle-free. And his skin is actually flawless! He doesn't look a day older than seventeen—though he does have a unique way about him—but he does just *seem* older.

They both walk past me, Bella flipping her hair and smiling while the guy gives me a look that sends my stomach to my feet. I feel almost dizzy after seeing him. It's as if he's looking at me to say he's going to rip me from limb to limb.

But no, I'm crazy to think that; it was just a look! In fact, as soon as he walks past me, I take my hand off of Stephanie's shoulder—which I've been longing to do since I put it on her—and run to the restroom. I puke, and I puke *violently*. I didn't eat much this morning. And I wouldn't ever buy Stephanie a bagel or get her a coffee like I had for Bella.

But it feels like when I start, I cannot stop.

"You alright man?"

"I feel like I'm about to throw up my intestines," I say between pukes, and I mean it jokingly, but it probably sounds serious with the way I'm gagging.

"Want me to get the nurse, man?"

I can only half make out the voice, but I see a pair of canvas sneakers. They're signed by *Walker Walking*, a local indie band that Michael and I went to see last summer. He had them sign his shoes because his band tee was already filled up with signatures.

"Michael?" I ask.

"It's me," he replies. "I saw you running in here."

Michael and I haven't exactly been on speaking terms since the homecoming dance. He, for reasons I can't relate to, has a huge crush on Stephanie. He has since we were in the fourth grade. Even though she has a rotten heart and is cruel and unkind, he likes her. I guess everyone deserves love at the end of the day.

But if me dating her ruins her for him, I'd be happy with that, too. Michael deserves better.

"I must have food poisoning or something," I mutter to him, saliva dripping out as I speak.

"Nah." Michael lets out a breath. "You just saw Bella with that weirdo. You're sick with jealousy. I know the feeling."

I feel a pang of guilt in my chest. *I know the feeling.* I had been so caught up in my anger and wanting to help Bella that I honestly hadn't thought of Michael for a second. It was only after I had already concocted my plan and gotten one foot into it that I even remembered Michael.

I open up the stall.

"Hey," I say to him.

"You look as pale as a fucking ghost," he says curtly, his curly hair bouncing as he shakes his head, "and I can't say I feel bad about it. You kinda deserve it, man."

"I'm the world's biggest asshole, aren't I?"

"Yeah."

And I'm smiling, but he doesn't laugh. He means it.

I sigh. "What if I told you I don't have feelings for Stephanie?"

Michael raises an eyebrow. "I'd say that dating her right in front of me—*and* Bella—is a pretty weird way of showing it."

I go over to the sink and splash some cold water on my face. When I look up at the mirror, I see that I really am as pale as a sheet of paper. How much should I tell Michael?

"Did you see what Stephanie did at the dance? To Bella?"

"What?" he asks, leaning against the pillar that separates the stalls. "What Stephanie did to Bella? What dance?"

I give my face a gentle slap and reach for the water bottle in my backpack. I finish the whole thing in one gulp, and I'm starting to feel a little better. The water bottle is actually a gift from Bella, before she was even my girlfriend. It's yellow, with a little sun printed on it.

"She humiliated her, man. She had this box, this weird ass box that sprayed her with all this gross stuff and—it was so mean, Michael. Stephanie is *awful*. I don't understand why you like her at all."

Michael seems to be considering this, but then speaks quickly in defense. "It's really hard for me to listen to you and take you seriously when you're literally *dating* her, Daven."

"I just want her to admit what she did to Bella. I want the full confession. If I can figure out how she did it, place her there, and get her to—I don't know, record her saying she did it, or even *texts* saying she did it—they will probably expel her. The school has a zero-tolerance bullying policy."

Michael raises his eyebrows. "You want her expelled?"

"Shh!" I hiss at him, looking toward the door. "I haven't even told Bella I'm doing this. She'd probably tell me not to or say she can fight her own battles—"

"So... maybe you shouldn't, and maybe she *can* fight her own battles."

"Do you think what Stephanie did was right?"

Michael is quiet. He shakes his head *no*. "She can be... intense."

"And you can still date her when she goes to the school across town." I splash my face with water again. "But Bella's life will be so much easier if Stephanie isn't here. And not *just* Bella. All the girls in our grade would celebrate. They'd play *Ding Dong! The Witch is Dead* on the announcements—"

"Watch it," Michael smiles, "I like Stephanie."

I turn to him. "But you shouldn't. You deserve better."

Michael looks down at his feet, frowning. "Maybe I do."

"Can I count on you?"

He looks up again. "Count on me for what?"

"Can I count on you to keep this a secret between us?"

He shakes his head. "Daven, I don't think you're thinking straight. Can you imagine what this might look like to Bella? She's already dating that weirdo. I think you doing this will make her go insane."

"It'll be worth it in the end," I reply, going toward the door. "I know it. Can I count on you?"

Michael takes in a deep breath, then shakes his head *yes*. I leave the restroom and go back toward my locker, where Stephanie is still leaning and twisting her hair. It'll all be worth it in the end.

I know it.

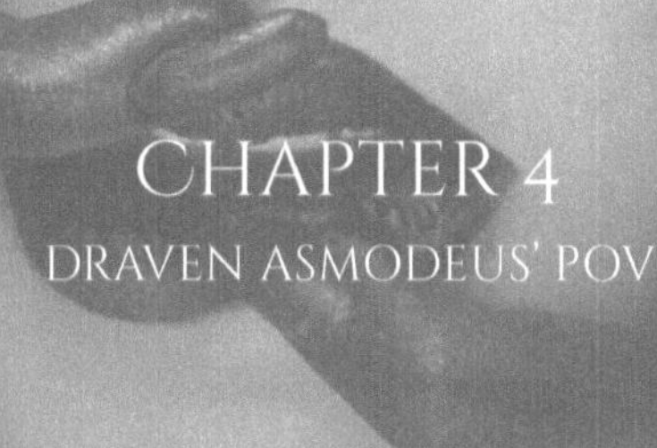

CHAPTER 4
DRAVEN ASMODEUS' POV

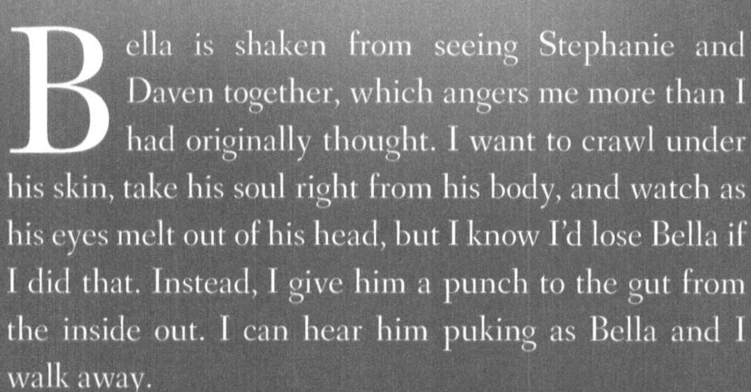

Bella is shaken from seeing Stephanie and Daven together, which angers me more than I had originally thought. I want to crawl under his skin, take his soul right from his body, and watch as his eyes melt out of his head, but I know I'd lose Bella if I did that. Instead, I give him a punch to the gut from the inside out. I can hear him puking as Bella and I walk away.

Now, with no interest in her classes when my

family is at stake, like the good girl she is, we're sitting on a park bench near her school. Her spirits are much higher than they were the night before, when she came home with the pills.

We didn't have anything like that in my day. Sometimes you'd eat the powder from crushed up herbs, and those would help you with some basic things, such as breaking a fever or throwing up poison. But the only remedies we had for the brain were the ones that opened a layer to the other dimension, where you could look at it through a magnifying glass. And even then, those were better consumed whole than in powder form. Those were my favorites.

"I want to help you," she says to me.

I can see fear in her eyes. As a demon, this is something I crave. But not with Bella. I don't want her to feel a negative emotion in her entire life, especially if it's one I have caused.

Bella is like a mirror. The chosen ones often are. It can lead them through a life of great sadness and anger. Like the entire world is out to get them, and it only gets worse the more resentful and hopeless they feel. Many of the chosen ones don't survive.

But sometimes the Chosen One is met with manifestations of happiness and luck. These ones don't last long, either. Because their riches always lead to something that will eventually break them. Maybe drugs, maybe worse. And once the descent happens, it happens quickly.

From what I can tell, Bella's family has done well

for themselves because they request little and expect less. I have suspicions about the mother, however, about the pots of herbs she simmers as she cooks, and the salt she pours at her door.

But as far as I can tell, Bella has never heard a word from her mother about their involvement in the Underworld. About their chosen status. That makes her the perfect victim—but I am weak. I pray that her and I can work together. That I don't have to turn her in order to get what I want.

So, I begin with a sob story. Maybe it's manipulation. But I'm a demon. There's much worse I can do.

"Your family reminds me of mine. You'd do anything to save them if they were in trouble, wouldn't you?"

She doesn't need to think about it. She nods. "Of course, I would."

"Because they'd do anything to save you, right? Even if you'd done something wrong?"

I can see a flashback swim across her eyes.

Yes, I know about Brick. I can feel her shame. I can see the scene written across her skin because it constantly eats at her. I'll use this to my advantage, without ever letting her know that I know.

She looks down at her hands, which are wrapped in mine as we sit at a picnic table near her school. "They would."

I nod. "Well. I did something wrong. When I was young. I was your age, probably. Maybe younger."

I was the exact same age, actually, that she was when she killed Brick.

"What'd you do?" she asks, eyes wide and innocent.

"I opened a door. It doesn't sound bad, but we had many warnings in our village. Humans in your generation call them *folktales*, but they were as real to us as the weather. We knew of demons who would rise to the surface, like weevils in rice, every thousand years. And it was time. So, we had new laws to follow," I tell her. "All doors remain open. All bodies of water are to be ignored. Don't look inside trees with holes."

"Those sound silly." She smiles. I love the way she lightens things with her smile.

"Yes, I thought so, too. They were hard rules to follow because they didn't make much logical sense. So, I ignored the most important one, *don't go swimming in the river at night*. The demons just needed a little of my life source to rise. And then... I let them take my father. The demons. I thought that would be enough for them. But then they came back for the rest of us and half the village."

"Because you went swimming? Draven, that's an innocent mistake. Not even a mistake! I don't know what I'd call it!"

I shrug. "It's a mistake that cost my family and I several millennia, and many of those were spent in horrendous pain and unbearable torture."

"Why did you give them your father?"

I try to think of a good answer.

"I thought they would stop with just him."

"Why did you think that?"

"They said they would."

"And they didn't?"

I sigh. "Demons lie. It's our favorite thing to do. We lie to anyone we can lie to. We lie when we're telling stories; we lie when we're telling secrets. We just *lie*."

Bella raises an eyebrow. "Do you lie to me?"

"You would know, Chosen One."

This answer satisfies her.

"Are they still being tortured?"

That's a loaded question. How might one define *torture?*

I nod. "They are."

She nods, too, as if she's made a decision. "Why me?"

I shrug. "I don't know why you were chosen. But you were."

"And what exactly am I supposed to do? Go to Lucifer's throne and beg for your family's release?"

I shake my head. "It's a little more complicated than that."

I hope to keep the secrets of its complication.

"Well, I need more information." Finally, she seems a little irritated. I know she's not stupid, and she knows I'm hiding, avoiding the real conversation. I feel her irritation itchy under my skin, the frustration thrusting itself under my skull.

"Okay. Well, first, we will try to find a portal. The Chosen One is supposed to be able to open it."

"Like you? Are you a chosen one?"

I shake my head. "That was different. That was when the layers between the portal were already thin. They aren't so thin right now."

"Well, I've never seen a portal. I don't know what it's supposed to look like."

"It's not like that. It'll be an element, a fire or water or earth or spirit or—"

"A spirit?"

"Like a place of worship. A place of prayer that you feel connected to."

She frowns, scratching in between her brows with one of her long-painted fingernails. "Yeah, religion and I haven't mixed well. I don't go to church."

"Unsurprising. Churches tell only lies. You probably know it's all bullshit."

She chuckles, still not looking up at me. "Maybe. I don't think my family has ever stepped foot inside a church."

"Maybe your mother knows." She snaps her head up, anger in her eyes, pushing past her mild irritation and growing full force.

"Don't say that."

I pretend to act surprised, as if I'm not actively trying to push her buttons. "Sorry, I didn't mean to offend you."

She softens.

"I just hope that if my mom knew, she would've told me. It feels like a pretty big thing to not tell your own daughter."

"Yes. Especially because it can mean so much danger, so much pain. You'd want to warn your child what might be coming for them, so that they could be safe. So, they wouldn't have to protect themselves."

I can see the guilt dancing across her skin again. If I can drive a wedge between her and her mother, her and her purest human connection, I might be able to convince her that what we have to do is warranted.

"You love your mom?" she asks.

"Of course, I do. And it's my fault that she's stuck down there."

"What kind of torture is she facing?"

Another truth I cannot tell. My mother is actually doing a lot of the torturing. After being asked for thousands of years if she was ready to succumb to the darkness, she finally agreed.

"Things I don't want to tell you, Bella. I don't want you to be scared to go down there."

"But then you are no better than my mom," she says sharply. "You don't want me to be protected or safe. I need all the information that I can get in order to be safe and protected."

I stifle a smile. My plan is working as expected. "I thought your mother doesn't know."

She looks back down at her nails. "She didn't. She *doesn't*. I just meant—"

"I will tell you all you need to know to be safe. We will find a portal. That part will be hard, not because it'll be hard to find, but because getting through the door isn't pleasant."

"How do you do it?"

"With a key. But the key is you. It's the worst thing you've ever done. The most horrendous thing that's ever happened to you. It'll play it back for you in the mirror, and if you can face yourself, if you can still push through, then you're in."

"That's what I'm worried about. What if I don't?"

I sigh. "You will get through it. We all do."

She rests her head on my shoulder, looking out at the rest of the park. The peaceful scenery in front of us. Swans swimming in the pond, trees blowing in the wind. This will all be madness soon enough.

"When do we start?" she asks.

"Now." I take her hand and guide her up, and we walk toward the thick trees of the forest. I can feel it all rushing through me now, a wild energy. This is working. It's finally going to work!

When my mother and sister join us up here, will they have a thirst for torture and pain? It has truly become an acquired taste of ours all those years down there.

And what if the door remains open?

Many will die. Bella's family may be amongst them, her friends.

Is lying to her worth my family coming back to me?

Save us, Draven! Help!

They feel my wavering heart. Okay, it's worth it.

CHAPTER 5
BELLA NOVA'S POV

Draven leads me toward the forest. I've been at this park very few times before. My mother said that during her childhood, this park was best known for tarantulas, hawks, and scorpions. For this reason, I avoided it like the plague. I wonder now what was true and what was a lie.

The trees are hanging low, and there is a break where five tree stumps sit in a circle. Draven looks at me, noticing my ring.

"You need to take that off," he says.

I clutch my hand defensively. "No way! My mom gave it to me."

Sure, I'm angry with her, but I would never take this ring off. That's what she told me when she gave it to me—never take it off.

He sighs, annoyed. "We cannot get through unless you take it off."

It's a pentagram, which would send many Christians clutching at their pearls. I'm confused and livid—there is so much to know, and I fear that Draven will only tell me the parts that are convenient to him.

"I thought pentagrams are like demonic signs or something. Don't they have something to do with the devil?"

Draven huffs, rolling his eyes. "No, Bella. It's quite the opposite, actually. The witches of your Earth are essential to keeping the demons *away*. The pentagram helps with that."

"Well, then why can you hold my hand? Why are you here?"

"It's not like throwing salt at a snail, Bella. Yours doesn't even look charged."

"Then why do I have to take it off?"

His lips tighten into a straight line.

"Obviously, no demon would wear a pentagram. If the demons see you, if they notice you, then they will crawl under your toenails and shoot out of your eyeballs."

My stomach turns. "What the fuck? That's sick!"

"Take the ring off, and you won't have to worry about it," he tells me.

I don't know if I believe him, but I'm too far in it now to say anything else. I take the ring off slowly. There's a low hanging branch, and I slip it on, giggling to myself about how it feels like I'm proposing to the tree.

A sadness then overwhelms me.

How silly! A teenage girl thinking about marriage as I descend into Hell.

I feel as though I've put myself in a spot that makes the future impossible, hopeless. I won't have a ring on my finger one day. I won't have a wedding, or be a bride, or have babies. I'll have to live with all of these mistakes I've made, with knowing that I've walked through the valleys of Hell.

Draven leads me toward the stumps, bringing me closer to the middle. Beetles are crawling all over the ground. It makes my skin crawl.

"Ew," I say, crinkling my nose. He lets a breath out, laughing.

"Yeah, maybe to you."

He stomps his foot, and the beetles scurry away. He then extends his hand toward me, and I follow his lead, both of us standing in the small space between the stumps.

"So... what now?"

He takes his hand, making it into a fist, and I cannot believe it. He crouches down really low and knocks. That's all, just knocks. He looks up at me. "Think you can do that?"

I roll my eyes. I wonder how many times I've almost, accidentally, fell into the depths of the Underworld because I was randomly knocking on things. I crouch down and give it one, two, three knocks.

In the blink of an eye, I'm in a dark and squishy room. It's like my nightmares all over again. The floor feels like it's made of jelly, like I could inadvertently sink through it at any given moment.

It's a deep purple down here, like an eggplant. The walls are shiny. I'm scared, but I'm also not surprised, given that I've been here before.

"Oh," I mumble to myself quietly. The sound echoes off the walls, which are made of the same substance.

"Get ready," he says, and all my emotions swarm over me at once. I'm feeling all the shame, all the guilt, and all the regret as I see his image projected onto the shiny purple wall, now solid and thick like glass. Like a mirror.

I see Brick, first as a baby coming out of his mother. Then, I watch as he grows up. He's a kid who doesn't seem to play well with others. But he's adorable, nonetheless, a child. I watch as his father and mother beat him mercilessly. I watch as he beats his girlfriends, or any woman who gets near him, mercilessly.

And I see as he kills his victims, ties them up, and assaults them. I see him chugging bottle after bottle of whiskey, throwing the glass at the wall and cutting his own hands and feet on the shards, sweeping them up, and looking at them confused the next morning.

And things get even weirder at one point. Suddenly, in these images of him drinking the dark liquor from glass bottles, there are more and more shadows in the room. They are looking over him. Trying to grab at him, trying to jump into him. And finally, one succeeds.

"Draven!" Someone is calling. "Save us!"

"Keep going, Bella! We're so close!"

Then there's me.

"Draven? Is that you?"

It's the sing-song voice of a little girl.

"I'm coming, Melanesia. Get ready!"

"Please, help!"

"Push, Bella! Don't waver! Don't succumb to the fear! Show that you are worthy!"

I'm watching it all happen, now through his eyes. Through the eyes of Brick, who was a broken child skipped over by the adults who were supposed to take care of him. I watch as he hurt other girls just like me.

And now, from his eyes, the eyes of a predatory demon. I'm watching this half-Brick, half-demon getting ready to pluck me like a chicken. The first time he saw me and... every detail. All of it. I'm disgusted just watching the stupidity. Like a lamb to the slaughter. I'm vulnerable and easy to take, and I would've been taken by this demon, forced to do something that Draven has been kindly guiding me into.

And I want to do this for him, but we're getting to

the end of the scene and... and *the end*. I shriek. I can't do it. I can't watch!

In the blink of an eye, we're back inside the forest.

Draven is red with fury, and I'm gasping for air.

"Water!" I cough. "I need some water!"

I point toward my backpack, which I had ditched near my ring, begging on my knees for Draven to grab the yellow water bottle hanging out of the pocket. He's livid as he stomps over to the bag, kicking it in the opposite direction. I bring my hands to my throat.

"What the fuck, Bella? You were almost there! Why did you stop?"

I point to my throat again, shocked that he kicked the bag. "Please! Water!"

My voice is hoarse. I feel sunburnt. I feel dizzy. I feel *nauseous*.

"I could hear my mother! I could hear my sister! Look what you've done! Now they're still in there, being tortured! And what if a guardian overheard them?! What if someone knows the veil is now thin and comes to kill me?"

"Draven!" I try again. My voice is nearly gone now.

He rolls his eyes, stomps over to the bag again, grabs the water bottle, and throws it at me. I open it quickly and lap at the water desperately. I fall back onto the ground, and a few stray beetles crawl toward my fingers. I jump up, and then the sun reflects off my ring.

But Draven sees where my eyes have gone and goes toward it, grabbing the ring from the tree.

"Why did you do that?" he demands again.

"Draven, give me that. It's mine!"

"My family is mine. And you stole them."

"I didn't steal anything!"

"You're the only one who can get them back, and you *refuse* to help!"

"I didn't refuse, Draven!" I scream at him. "That was my first fucking time in the depths of Hell, having to watch something so horrifying, something I've worked desperately to erase from my memory. Not to mention that you *didn't mention* that demons have been trying to get me for years!"

Draven is silent. Then he rolls his eyes, walking toward the park. "Fucking duh, Bella. You need to figure some shit out before we try this again. I don't think you understand any of this."

He's too far gone for me to say anything to him.

"Then help me understand," I whisper to myself. Because it's abundantly clear that Draven is hiding something.

CHAPTER 6
DAVEN PORTER'S POV

Bella hasn't been in any of her classes today.

But I know she was at school. One, I saw her this morning. Two, she left something in my locker.

We exchanged combinations before we even started dating. She lost her Literary Composition text-book, and we'd been sharing the same one ever since. She would put it in there after she took the class, first period, then I'd grab it for fourth period.

Somewhere in between when I'd put my geography book back at the end of yesterday, and this morning when I took out my math textbook for my first period class, she had put a yellow rain jacket in my locker with a little note.

This is for CeCe. I heard her asking your mom for one.

There was a tiny duck embroidered on the pocket. It was shiny, the rubber vinyl material making squeaky noises as I observed it. I put it straight into my backpack before Stephanie could see.

Normally, I'd leave her alone, let her have the independence she deserves. But that's if I hadn't seen her with that freak this morning. I don't trust him. And though I fell for Bella quickly, she fell for me quickly, too. I worry about her, which is ironic. I don't worry about myself because I know that what I felt was real. But how could she have known, said it back to me so quickly?

When I finally spot Bella, she has her backpack flung over her shoulder, and she is quickly walking toward the library at school. She has a twig in her hair, and she looks like she's been crying. I want to reach out to her, but Stephanie swoops in out of nowhere.

"So, *babe*, should I come over later? I'd love to meet Jackie."

"Jackie?" I roll my eyes, "My mom?"

"Duh, Madame Mayor!" Stephanie is popping and chewing a piece of gum, and it disgusts me.

"Why?" I'm laughing because Stephanie has a

thousand and one surprises. You'd think one or two of them would be, at least, good surprises. But none of them have been thus far. I look back toward the library, and Bella is gone. I sigh, defeated.

"Just wanna see what it's like living a life of luxury," she says, reaching her hand toward my left thigh. I smack it away. She huffs. "What? I'm your girlfriend now."

"I never said that," I hiss at her, going toward my locker. "We're dating, but I never said that."

"Why are you like this, Daven?" She chases after me, then leans against the locker next to mine. "What's your problem? You don't still have feelings for her, right?"

"No, of course not," I lie through my teeth, though I say it sarcastically. Then an idea comes to me. I discreetly take my phone out from my pocket and put it into my locker, hitting the recording app. I then press the record button and shut the locker. "Not after what you did to her."

Stephanie raises an eyebrow. "You think it was me?"

"I *know* it was you," I say with a fake enthusiastic tone. "That was so funny! How did you come up with that? How did you get everything to explode out of it? It hit Bella right in the face. How?"

She smirks. "I just had some nerds from the rocket club help. They powered it up, basically made it into a bomb. I just had to tell Bella that it's my way of saying sorry—"

I'm almost too angry to conceal my feelings, but I press on. My face tightens, and I can see Stephanie watching the rage cross my face. "You? Sorry?"

"She wouldn't have opened it otherwise, duh!"

I pause, taking another deep breath.

"Okay. Who else helped you?"

"I'm actually, like, really smart, Daven. I just needed the nerds to draw up the plans, and I did everything else myself. You should've seen her face when it hit her. You only got to see the aftermath of my conniving work."

"Wow," is all I say back. Wow is actually an understatement. This girl is truly *evil*.

The bell rings, and Stephanie looks up, giving me another smile. "Gotta go! See you later?"

"Sure," I mutter. I watch as she walks away, going up the stairs toward her Spanish class. Then I open my locker again and grab my phone, ending the recording. "Evil bitch."

I shove the phone into my pocket and head toward the principal's office.

But that's when I see him.

Hunched over as he walks, his feet drag toward the entrance of the school. He looks nefarious in his manner alone. The energy he exudes is equal parts intimidating and mystifying.

The principal's office can wait.

I throw my backpack over one shoulder and wait until there's a large enough distance between us, then I follow him. I sneak behind pillars as we exit the school, and eventually, I lurk behind trees as we go toward the nearby park.

Why is he going to the park?

If I hadn't seen Bella go into the library, I'd be worried that he'd buried her out there. This guy is *that* weird, *that* creepy. Instead, I see him head toward the creek.

I stand behind a tree, about twenty-five feet away. I'm careful to not make a sound.

Draven reaches down, grabs a handful of water, and throws it into the air.

And I'm shocked! The water freezes, mid-air.

"I need to speak with Melanesia," he says to the frozen water.

"What did you do to deserve Hell?" a bellowing voice asks.

"Show me my sins!" Draven says back in an annoyed tone. He says it casually, as enthusiastically as one might say, "Check my account balance" or "Connect me to customer service."

Quietly, I creep closer. The water has spread itself thin, displaying a larger-than-life version of a scene. It's Draven, but he's wearing clothes that someone might've worn centuries ago. It's a smock, with a sword on his hip. And he's using a smaller knife to cut something.

As I look closer, I see what that something is. It's a boy, who looks just like him. His eyes are blackened, his body nearly blue. Draven is carving symbols all over his body. I see it, too, from the perspective of the body. Then I listen as the water vision of Draven speaks.

"I sacrifice thee to Lucifer in exchange for riches and food."

I throw my hands over my mouth.

"Where are you?" a new voice asks. I see on the screen a little girl. She can't be much older than CeCe. But she looks eerie, a little off. I can't quite make out what it is about her, not from this far away.

"I'm going to be there soon. Prepare yourselves."

"How are you going to get here?" the little girl asks again.

"I have found the Chosen One, Melanesia."

Melanesia? That must be her name.

"Mother grows weaker," Melanesia whispers.

"Where is your father?"

"Away. Trying to figure out how to get up there like you did. He is furious about your departure, brother."

Brother?

"He can come up here whenever he wants. I don't care. I just want you two spared. I want you two up here." Draven tenses his brows as he continues to speak, like he's worried about something.

"He is thirsty for the blood of the humans."

"There is plenty of that up here. For now, I am only bringing the Chosen One to get you and mother. Do not tell your father."

"And what if I do, brother?"

"Then I will have the Chosen One banish you

right back to the Underworld, and you will have to suffer down there without mother and I."

"My father is a royal man. I will not suffer," Melanesia protests.

"You *will* suffer without your mother. Even you know that."

"He will just come up to the surface and bring her back."

"He cannot come up to the surface now, not without the Chosen One." Draven seems awfully confident in his words.

"And you trust that I won't turn her over?"

"I don't trust you as far as I can throw you, Melanesia."

"So, why do you come to save me from Hell, brother?"

"Because I sacrificed a brother once to meet Lucifer. Now I will sacrifice a lover to fix my mistake." Draven lowers his head, a sense of shame washing over him.

A lover?

I take a step back. And a tree branch breaks.

"Will I like it up there, brother?"

"Hello?" Draven looks back into the forest, then back at the water. "An animal. Yes, sister, you will love it. Trust me. Please."

"Though you don't trust me?"

"Yes."

"Fine. Hurry."

"Don't tell your father."

"I won't."

And then the water drops down into the river. I turn around and run. As my feet finally hit asphalt, a car just starting up from the stop sign hits me. It's not moving fast, and I'm not in too much pain, but I hit my head against the hood of the car.

What did I just witness?

CHAPTER 7
BELLA NOVA'S POV

I can't stop seeing it.

I regret, immensely, having agreed to do anything with Draven. And still, I wonder if Draven is even real.

"Is it possible that... I mean, can we talk more about hallucinations?"

Dr. Schultz nods, taking a sip of his coffee and putting his pen down.

"Ms. Nova... I think I do need to acknowledge

the irregularity of this circumstance. Are you struggling with the medication? With the current dosage? I do have flexibility in my schedule for instances like this, but I wasn't expecting to see you until next week."

I scratch an itch behind my neck.

I can't stop seeing it.

Lamb to a slaughter, lamb to a slaughter, lamb to a slaughter. And so many times in my life, I *was* the lamb to a slaughter. There are so many things becoming abundantly clear to me as I think about it more. That teacher's assistant that my mom had gotten fired—was she also a demon, possessed? Are female demons gentler?

And what about the other boys? What about all the strange instances in my life, where strangers got a bit too close or waiters lingered a bit too long, and my mom barked or snapped or pulled me up by the elbow to lead me away? Were they also just demons trying to get something from me?

What do they want?

Except I'm worried that I *do* know what they want. Draven has made it clear that he wants his family released from the Underworld, but the research I did at the library a few hours ago doesn't make it seem that simple.

Portals are easy to get through once they're open. For millennia, people have been sent to the depths of Hell. They're packed in there, like sardines in a can, ready to burst out of the first open portal. How did

Draven even get out without more people escaping? How had the other demons?

There are some things they know that we don't. They, the demons that is, know the workarounds that humans cannot understand. They know, too, the politics of Hell. The way they must please their lord, Lucifer.

But do they know what we know? Do they know about how we use pentagrams for protection, how yellow and color and florals and happiness are their kryptonite, how a little essence of lemon may drive them mad? Do they know this? Are they prepared for it?

I'm pedaling through these thoughts, and Schultz is still looking at me, head tilted. He wants me to answer him. But I don't know how.

Because even through all this research and all these realizations, I'm hoping with my entire being that this is all just a manifestation of my guilt. That I've only broken through my own consciousness and gone into psychosis because I just feel *awful* for killing Brick. I'm hoping that I created this demon thing, this whole story, just to make everything make sense.

I'm hoping I'm just insane.

"I just needed someone to talk to. Maybe the pills aren't working."

Schultz nods. "Okay. Tell me how you have been feeling over the past few days."

How I've been feeling? It's less about how I feel and more about where I've been, what I've seen. Me, through the eyes of a man who intended to kill me—to do much worse, quite frankly.

"I had... a bad experience in my past."

He nods again. "I've noticed some signs of a possible past trauma. A complex version of this can often be mixed up with Bipolar Disorder."

"Sure, well... I was this way before it happened. But this didn't help, of course."

He shifts his weight, crossing his legs. "Do you want to tell me more about this experience, Bella?"

Don't tell him anything, Bella.

I gulp. Draven is here. When did he come back? Where is he?

Schultz doesn't move an inch. He's still waiting for my answer.

He'll lock you up. If you say a word, he will lock you up. Not in the loony bin, Bella. In jail. In prison. He has to tell on you if you did something that hurt someone else. You killed someone, Bella. You're on the run. Do not say a word.

I turn my head, looking behind me. It sounds like he's right behind me, whispering into my neck. I can feel his breath. But there's no one there.

"Bella?" Schultz asks as I look back and forth frantically.

I'm breaking out into a cold sweat. I can feel the beads dripping down the front of my head.

"I'm hearing things..."

Stop, Bella.

Schultz doesn't say anything for a moment. I reach

toward my bag, grabbing the little vial of lemon essence from the front pocket. I find the lip and pour out a few drops onto the top of my hand. Then I take my index finger and rub it on the back of my neck, the top of my forehead, the corner of my eyes, and the center of my wrists.

What are you—?

His voice grows quieter.

"Are you hearing things right now, Bella?" Schultz asks.

"Not anymore," I respond, holding the vial up. "This helps."

He smiles. "What helps, Bella? What is the voice saying? Is it in the room, or is it in your head?"

"Both. He's in the room, and he's in my head, if I can be honest with you. He's everywhere. I can only get rid of him with this."

"What is it?" he asks again. "May I see it?"

And I hand him the bottle. He gives it a little sniff.

"It's an oil."

"Lemon," he says, "is that correct?"

I nod my head. "It helps. Yellow helps. Flowers help. Feeling happy helps. Thinking happy thoughts and having happy memories help."

Schultz is quiet again. He leans back against his chair, wondering. I see him look toward the phone on his desk. If he has to admit me, fine. I hope he does.

"Bella, how long have you been hearing this voice?"

"Since the nightmares began."

"And when did the nightmares begin?"

"When we moved."

"And when did you move?"

"When the bad thing happened." At this point, I'm whispering. Not because I want to, but because I'm running out of steam. I'm running out of energy. I'm going to cry soon, and I'm going to completely break down. Everything that I've tried to shove down, everything that I've ignored, everything that I've numbed... they're all here at the surface.

I've made some awful decisions. I've made some big mistakes. And whether Draven is real or not, I'm being punished for them. I pray that this punishment is one of my own creations. I pray that Draven isn't actually real.

"What do you think we should do about this, Bella?" he asks.

"Can you send me somewhere?"

"Yes."

"I see him, too. I see things, Dr. Schultz. I'm seeing things and hearing things."

"We can find a safe place for you. I'm going to call your parents, but first, I'm going to call my assistant." Schultz gets up and goes toward his desk. His shadow jumps against the wall, the lamp illuminating him. But his shadow straightens, stands tall though he hunches. Then Schultz looks back at me. He throws the glass vial of lemon essence onto the ground. His eyes are completely black.

"Doctor—"

"Bella, why aren't you listening to me?" he asks. It is Draven's voice.

"What are you doing? Are you hurting him?"

"Of course not, Bella. I'm not hurting him, I swear. He was going to send you away, and I need you."

"Draven, please. You aren't real. None of this is real."

"If none of this is real, then you'll be opening your eyes in a mental hospital soon enough. If none of this is real, dance along in this adventure for fun. Okay?" He smiles a creepy smile. I grab my bag and bolt toward the office door, leaving before Schultz's assistant can even ask for payment.

I get a block away before Draven is at my side again.

"I didn't hurt him," he swears.

"What are you doing here?" I ask, crying. "This is a big deal for me, Draven. You've lived in Hell for five millennia, and I've only been living in Hell for a week. You have no idea how hard it was to see all of that played back to me. I needed to talk to someone!"

Draven shrugs. "I wish you would've told me. I wish you didn't keep it a secret. I could've sat with you and coached you, and made sure he didn't send you away."

"Maybe I *need* to go away." I stop in the middle of the sidewalk, tears in my eyes as I look up at Draven. "Maybe I *am* insane."

Draven sighs, shifting his weight from one foot to the other. "Okay, if that's true, and you admitted to that man that you were seeing things and hearing things, what did you think would happen?"

"He'd send me away. To a hospital. Where I could get better."

"So, then you'll wake up there. If this is all a nightmare, then just let it play out."

I shake my head. "It cannot be that simple, Draven."

Draven sighs again. "He'll only be knocked out for another hour or two—"

"Knocked out?!"

"You told him you were hearing and seeing things, and then you left. He's going to open his eyes and only remember that you were there and then gone. He's going to call your parents. The police, even. So, we have to go to the forest and do this now."

"What?"

"Now. Then you can go to the hospital, and they'll tell you that this was all a delusion or whatever. Okay? Then you'll never have to see me again."

I frown. So, that's it? Then we'll be over? I'll never see Draven again? I thought he loved me. I shake my head.

"Whatever, Draven. Take me to the stupid forest."

He grabs my hand and yanks me so hard that I worry my shoulder is going to pop out of the socket. I'm not much of an athlete, not a runner by any means, but we spring through the streets and toward the woods.

Now *these* woods, I've never been in. They're off

the highway. An easy place to kill someone and hide their body, if that's what Draven plans to do.

This time, he pulls me toward a small creek that runs over sharp, jagged rocks. I see a sewage tunnel down the current, and the water looks mossy, murky, gross. He steps into the water and pulls me in. My shoes are soaked! I can smell the sewage!

He crouches down, pulling my hand. Then I knock.

I'm in the squishy room again. I take a deep breath and shift myself, trying to find my balance and looking for the mirror. It's behind me.

Luckily, the first part goes by fast. I've seen it before. I haven't *stopped* seeing it. And then I see the rest. I see my face as I kill a man. I see, I hear, I smell, I *feel* the last moments of Brick's life.

"We're in!" Draven smiles.

He is inches away from an evil laugh. The walls begin to come toward us, the ceiling and floor closing together like magnets. Draven grabs my hand. We are submerged in this squishy jelly, and I feel all the breath, all the life, leave my body.

I can't see a thing! I can't hear a thing! I can only feel things around me. I feel elbows. I feel mouths. I feel other parts of bodies. And I feel hands grabbing at me, getting tangled in my hair. I am trapped in a pile of bodies.

Draven squeezes tighter, pulling me through them, and I try to keep my mouth shut. I feel things crawling in every crevice. My ears, my nose, my navel, under my shirt, up my skirt. I want to scream, but I also don't want to give anything the opportunity to get inside my throat.

"Draven! You came for us!" The small child's voice is right in front of me. "Who is *she*?"

I realize now that I couldn't see a thing because I had my eyes squeezed tightly shut. I open them now.

I'm standing in a room that looks like the inside of a sunset. Everything is red and orange; everything is light and heat. There is a little girl, with long black nails like Draven used to have. Another woman is standing there, long matted hair, eyes filled with black, and nails so long that they curl.

"Who is she?" the taller woman asks.

"Chosen One," Draven says quickly, grabbing both of them by the hand. He puts the little girl up onto his back and pulls the tall woman in closer. "No time to explain. Be quiet as we walk through the portal. Don't say a word."

"Hi!" the little girl greets me. The more I look at her, the more terrifying she is. She reminds me of CeCe, but only at first. The height, the pigtails. But this one has no lips. She only has sharp teeth, no nose, and huge eyes like an owl.

"Hi," I say back, and as soon as I open my mouth, I absorb a taste so foul that I fear I might puke.

"Don't," Draven says to me, grabbing my other hand. He begins to pull us, running faster than when we ran toward the portal, and I shut my eyes again, praying that he will guide me. Praying that if he really doesn't love me, he'll at least not leave me down here.

"Follow them! Follow them! Follow them!" I hear voices repeat as we move through the crowd of bodies again.

"Get away from us!" the tall woman screams.

"Come with us! We're going to Earth," the little girl cheers. "We will get our revenge. Come with us! Come with us! Come with us!"

And I'm too terrified to say a single word.

"Knock, Bella! Knock!" Draven is screaming at the top of his lungs, and only now do I realize that I had also blocked out the noises of the bodies the first time through. All I hear are moans of pain, shrieks, screams, curses. Draven squeezes my hand, and I reach my hand out, looking for something to knock on. "Open your eyes!"

I do. All around me are bodies, bruised and bloody, faces in horror, jaws slack, eyes gouged, mouths cut open. There are hands grabbing onto my legs, hanging onto my elbows, and holding onto strands of my hair. And then, finally, over my shoulder, I see a river rock. I knock.

And just like Heaven, I hear the sounds of birds chirping and the creek moving over the rocks. I see the sunlight. I feel the California air. But most terrifying of all, I feel weightless as the dozens of bodies who held onto me, pulled me down into the pile, are now running at the speed of light away from the creek.

"Some got out—" I begin to say, but I can already tell that Draven doesn't care.

He's hugging his mother, kissing her head, crying at her feet. She doesn't look the same as she did in the Underworld. Here, she looks like a normal woman. A mom. She's wearing a button-down dress made from old cotton material. Her hair is long and curly down her back. Her eyes are blue.

But the little girl looks the same. I scream.

She tilts her head, smiling with her terrifying mouth. "That's not very nice. I thought humans are supposed to be good. Maybe *they* should be in Hell instead."

She reaches a hand toward me, her claws becoming longer.

"Stop it, Melanesia," Draven says, and she does. "She's from a chosen family. You cannot send her to Hell, but she can sure send you back.

"Oh, no," Melanesia smiles wider, "she cannot send me back. I am half human. I am half her. I am half true demon. I am half you. She cannot send me back."

"Am I done?!" I look at Draven, stomping my feet. "Have you gotten your use out of me?"

He rolls his eyes. "Dramatic, Bella. You are being dramatic. But yes, you are done. You have gotten your use out of me, evidently, so I have gotten my use out of you."

He turns back to his mother, kissing her hands and apologizing profusely. But the mother continues to stare at me.

"Humans are disgusting," she spits.

So, no thank-yous are in order, I suppose?

"What about those things that escaped, Draven?"

"You don't have to worry about that," Melanesia says, reaching her hand out to me. "Will you show me what a human looks like?"

I pull my hand away. "No."

"Humans are supposed to be good," she sings.

"Bye, Draven," I ignore her and say to him. He doesn't even look at me. I grab my backpack, take one last look at the family, and run away. I don't know where home is, but one way or another, I'm going to find it.

CHAPTER 8
DAVEN PORTER'S POV

Bella's father hangs up the phone as her mother paces back and forth.

"Well," he says, "that was a psychologist named Dr. Shultz—"

"Schultz," I correct. "I know him. I suggested that she go to him."

Her mother frowns, turning toward her husband. "So, she's going to therapy without telling us, too?

Secret boyfriends, secret psychologists? What else is she hiding?"

"Listen," Mr. Nova grabs his wife by the shoulders so that she'll stop pacing, "she left his office just a few hours ago. He had a fit. He thinks he passed out or had a seizure, and Bella just *left him there*."

"She was probably having flashbacks from—" Mrs. Nova looks over at me, and then back at Mr. Nova. "You know."

"Well, she told him she was having auditory and visual hallucinations. He was just getting ready to call us, ready to call an ambulance. He highly recommends that we institutionalize her for a little bit, at least for the time being until she feels better."

"Auditory hallucinations? Visual hallucinations?" Again, Mrs. Nova looks away from her husband, then back at me, then back at her husband. "Can I talk to you in the other room, dear?"

I get the hint.

"I'm about to head home," I tell them. "I just thought you all should know that this Draven guy is... not good. He's not good at all. I can't really explain to you how not good he is. And Bella has been seeing him, and I'm scared, and I have... I feel like I'm going crazy. And I just thought you guys could help. I'm worried for her."

Mrs. Nova squints her eyes and tightens her lips together in a flat line. "What did you see, Daven?"

"What?" I ask, my voice a little shaky. I don't know *what* I saw. I'm confused about what I saw, of course.

Maybe I saw him having a video call with his sister, and the run-in with the car just jumbled all of my memories. What I thought I saw is much stranger than what makes sense. I trace the stitch above my eyebrow that I got at urgent care.

"You saw something," Mrs. Nova says, coming toward where I'm sitting at their breakfast bar. "Tell me what you saw."

"I don't know what I saw." I shrug, "I can't be sure. I hit my head pretty bad when I collided with the car."

But she just shakes her head. "I don't care if you sound crazy, Daven. Tell me what you think you saw."

I sigh.

"I think I saw Draven talking to his little sister or something."

"How?"

I let out a bigger sigh. "Via... creek water."

"Oh, God," Mr. Nova puts his hand on his chest, "you don't think..."

"And what did they talk about?" Mrs. Nova puts her hand out in front of her husband's face, indicating that he needs to shut his mouth.

"Hell," I whisper.

"Hell?"

"I think Hell," I repeat, "or the Underworld. I'm sorry, Mrs. Nova. I'm just tired, and my mom is freaking out about the concussion, and I feel like I was just having weird dreams—"

"Give him a ride," Mrs. Nova demands her husband, "and start looking for—"

"Mom?" Someone's calling from the outside. The front door swings open, and here comes Bella, out of breath, eyes swollen with tears again. "Daven?"

"Bella!" I stand up, arms outstretched as I move toward her. She flinches away.

"Take him home, *now*," Mrs. Nova repeats.

Bella's father grabs his car keys and gives his daughter a kiss on the head before heading toward the front door. I follow. Bella won't even look at me.

"Bella, I know you're mad at me," I whisper to her, "but all of this will make sense at school tomorrow. I got Stephanie to admit what she did, and they'll probably suspend her and—"

Bella finally looks at me, eyes wide, and she's about to say something when Mrs. Nova takes her under her arm and begins to lead her away. "Sorry, Daven. We have bigger things to worry about."

CHAPTER 9
BELLA NOVA'S POV

"I've had a long day," I tell her, falling onto my bed and folding my arms. I realize now that I've lost one of my nails. I'm upset that I'm even upset about this.

"Yeah, sounds like it," my mom says sarcastically. She sits next to me and folds her arms, too. "So, tell me about your demon boyfriend."

I roll my eyes. "What? Did Dr. Schultz call?"

It's then that I realize I'd never told Schultz about

the demon being my boyfriend. I snap my head to look at my mother. She is giving me an all-knowing look.

"Yeah, I know everything. I know more than you even think I could know. Guess how much I know, and know that I know double that."

"Okay," I unfold my arms, "then tell me what you know. Did you know that I'm the Chosen One?"

She rolls her eyes. "Less of *the* Chosen One, and more of *one* of the chosen ones."

"Why didn't you tell me?"

She sighs, unfolding her arms now. She gets down onto the floor, onto her knees. She looks up at me from there, resting her head on her arms. "I wanted you to have a normal life."

"Pretty normal!" I throw my hands up in the air. "I kill a man before I can even drive, force you all to move to a different state, date a demon—"

"Considering that all the women before you have had run-ins with death, demons, and more... it's as normal as I would've hoped." She smiles, then frowns. "I wonder if I should've told you more. About what it means to be a chosen one. There are a few families in this town who are descendants of chosen ones. But they all... well, I wouldn't say they were *lucky*. But most of them had a kid or two, all boys, and felt themselves blessed. Having a girl is the trouble."

"Great," I roll my eyes, "so I was born a mistake, too?"

My mom shakes her head. "Of course not. You are no mistake, Bella. Women descendants have the gift, which is terrifying in its own right. But the sons take more after their fathers, who don't."

I pause.

"What would you have told me, then? If you *did* decide to tell me?"

My mom crosses her fingers and closes her eyes. "That you are a mirror, Bella. Whatever you feel, people around you will reflect. The boys you fall in love with fall so hard for you because you fall so hard for them. And I'd tell you that... you'll attract demons. You'll attract bad people your whole life, my love, and you have to be stronger than them. And I'd tell you... that you should always wear a perfume that makes you happy, and whatever clothes make you feel best, and that you should do what you love and be with who you love so you can live your happiest life because, that way, all you'll do is attract happiness."

I give her a half smile. "Sounds like what any mom would tell her daughter."

She nods. "Except the mirror part, I hope."

"I guess I should've seen that on my own." I wipe a tear from my eye. "I'm sorry for being mad at you, Mom. You guys sacrificed so much to move here for me."

She gives me a full smile now.

"I was happy to move back here, Bella. Once I knew you weren't safe there, I was happy to move back here. It really is safer in this town. I know four elderly women in this town who never had children. They are descendants of chosen ones, and they still practice daily. There are three women my age, who were in my coven when I was a child—"

"You were in a coven?"

My mom sighs.

"You know, Bella. The layers between Heaven and Hell and Earth are all very thin. At any given moment, there are demons beating against the floor of Earth just waiting to get in. There are women doing the thankless jobs of keeping those demons at bay while battling the demons up here—the *humans* up here, too."

I gulp. Mom says she knows everything, times two. Does she know that I carried up ten, maybe fifteen, demons when I came back from Hell? Does she know that I was there? I'm not angry with her anymore, but I'm fearful. I'm fearful for the disappointment, the pain that's coming.

"I didn't know," I simply say, looking down at my hands that were sitting on my lap.

"Daven is in a descendant family," my mom tells me.

My head snaps up, eyes wide. "He is?"

"Yes," my mom nods, "Jackie was in my coven. We were close friends. She called me as soon as she met you. I knew you were lying about where you were, but I knew you were safe, too. The iron fences. The pentagrams. You may not have seen them, but Jackie runs a tight ship."

"Does Daven know?"

My mom shakes her head. "I don't think so."

"Huh," I mutter, "small world."

"Small world, maybe. But the Underworld is large, and the skyscraper that is Heaven is even bigger—"

"I know," I interrupt her. And I say it quickly with no other context, fearing her questions.

"You know?" she asks.

"I know."

"Know what?"

"How large the Underworld is."

Mom gets up off the floor.

"How do you know that?" She looks down at my hand. "Where's my ring?"

I put my face in my hands. "He took it."

"*Who* took it?"

"Draven?"

"Daven?"

"No!" I cry out, removing my hands and putting them at my sides. "The demon. Draven."

My mom puts her hand to her mouth. "That was the last one we had. You lost the amulet when you were younger—"

"The amulet?"

"That was the only thing that could stop an invasion, and you *lost* it, so they forged you that ring so you'd never be tempted through the Gates of Hell and—"

"How was I supposed to know?"

"I told you to never take it off!" she screams. "Why didn't you listen?"

My mother has never been this angry with me before. Her face is beet red, and she is inches from my face. Suddenly, we hear a scream coming from outside.

"What was that?" I ask.

"Oh, God!" She puts her hand to her mouth. "What did you do, Bella?"

CHAPTER 10
DRAVEN ASMODEUS' POV

"I'm terribly sorry that this must be the way we meet." I hold my hand out to Bella's mother, and she pulls her hand behind her back.

"What did you do to my daughter?" she demands.

"He didn't do anything that she didn't want to do," my own mother replies. She crosses her arms and sits on the bed. "Listen, mother to mother, let's have a talk."

Bella's mother opens her eyes wide, and she tightens her lips. "Who are you?"

"Draven, I think you should go," Bella says. Her lips are quivering.

I do as she requests. I feel the love that I have for her pouring from my heart. I can almost see her face change, see her body reacting to this love. She feels it, too.

I can feel her mother glaring at me, her eyes burning the back of my head. I flip around.

"Bella," she says, "he's manipulating your feelings. You must resist."

Bella shrinks away, jumping onto her bed. She shoves her head against her pillow.

"Listen," my mother says, "my son made a mistake long ago. He has corrected that mistake today, but now my husband—"

"My step-father is a very powerful demon," I jump in, cutting my mother off. "He wants her and my half-sister back. Bella accidentally let out a few demons when we saved my mother and sister, and those demons brought with them some of her essence, and they have opened the portal."

"I have to make some calls." Mrs. Nova begins to head out of the room. "Draven, you come with me."

"No," I state, "I need you all to come with *me*. The demons are escaping Hell at an alarming rate. Things are bad, and I acknowledge that most of this is my fault. I think Bella will be highly sought after, and we need to keep her safe somewhere. I should carry her down to Hell—"

"Ha!" her mother snorts. "Fat chance, buddy. We can handle this up here."

"Listen," my own mother shakes her head. "Bella isn't safe here. My husband knows that she helped release me. He is going to be looking for her. You all need to find somewhere safe to stay."

"Give her the ring back." Bella's mother looks at me, ignoring my mother. I dig it out of my back pocket and hand it back to Bella, who sobs.

"Lucifer's army is rising. With all due respect, we need to get you all somewhere safe."

"I will *never* step through the Gates of Hell *again*," her mother repeats. "Bella, put this on. It'll help you resist him."

Her mother digs in the closet, pulling out a yellow shawl. It's hard for me to look at Bella as she wraps herself in it.

"Look." I start to speak louder, turning to her mother. "I did some bad things. I am a demon. I spent so much time in the Underworld that I don't know left from right, and I do crave blood. I do crave torture. I do crave destruction. But I have resisted every urge because your daughter is special, and I love her, and—"

"Stop!" Mrs. Nova puts her hand up. "Stop right now."

"No!" I shout, and my eyes fill with fire. "She is in grave danger. Swallow your pride and—"

"This may come as a shock," she continues, "but

we have been doing just fine up here without double agents. Bella will be safe here because I'm here, and because there are dozens of women on this land who are probably already fighting the army off, and—"

"No." My mother shakes her head and stands up, going toward Bella's mother. Bella's mother steps away. "I was never meant to go to Hell. I was a good mother. I was a good person. My son made an awful choice, took my *other* son from me, and... it was like I didn't belong on Earth anymore because it brought too much pain."

"He did what?" Bella sits up on her bed. I feel a coldness all over my body. I *did* tell her that demons lie, after all. I did.

"My son made mistakes, but he is righting them. I had no doubt that he'd free us, but I thought it would end in death and destruction for your kind. Your daughter changed him. She changed his heart. Believe me, he wants to help you."

"Demons lie," her mother says quickly. Bella nods.

"I am no demon. I am a mother," my mother reaches out her hand. "I am truly good. I am."

I see Mrs. Nova considering it.

"Please, just go," she says. "You'll want to leave, trust me. I'm going to fill the entire house with the essence of lemon, and you are going to feel like you're choking. *Go.*"

CHAPTER 11

BELLA NOVA'S POV

"**M**om," I repeat. She is drawing pentagrams up and down my arm. I can hear the screams from the streets, and I smell ash. "Are you sure we're safe here?"

"I have been preparing for this my whole life," my mother says. She pulls out a pair of my pajamas and puts them on my lap. "Go take an Epsom salt bath. Rub the rocks into your skin. Then dress. You need rest. It's harder for them to possess you if you are asleep."

"Mom, please let me help," I plead, pushing the pajamas back. She shakes her head.

"I need to make some calls."

"I'm sorry, Mom!" I plead again.

She gives me a soft smile but pulls out her phone. I see my dad's picture pop up across the phone screen. She answers, and I can hear more screaming. She frowns, like she's about to cry, and then leaves my room, shutting the door behind me. I hear scraping against the floor. When I go to my door and try to push it gently, it won't budge.

She blocked me in!

I let out a breath and tap my foot.

If I really am the Chosen One, I cannot be stopped by a locked door!

I squeeze my eyes shut and think of Draven. I think of when I first met him, and our first time together, and our first kiss. And poof! Just like magic, here he is, sitting on my bed.

"Your mother is just about as stubborn as mine," he says.

He has a coy side smile, even though the world is crumbling outside. It's unfortunate that it still makes my heart skip a beat. It's clear as day just how awful he's been to me these past few days. But wouldn't I do the same for my mother? She certainly did the same for me.

"Draven," is all I can manage to say.

He stands up, closing the distance between us.

"I'm sorry for how I acted today, Bella. But I was stressed about this, okay? I needed to get my mother up here, and I needed to get my sister up here, and I don't even know where she is now—"

"I get it," I cut him off. "I wouldn't do the same thing for Ace, necessarily. But I'd do the same for my mother. And she did, basically, do the same thing for me. But why did you lie about all of this?"

"It felt like it was worth the risk for me," he says, shrugging, "but I'm sorry."

I nod. "Am I safe here?"

"Probably not."

I sigh.

"My mother told me to take a salt bath."

"That's probably a good idea. That and lemon repulse demons. No one will grab onto you when I take you down there," he replies. "I'll wait here."

My eyes widen, and I shake my head. "No, no, no. I'm not going down there with you—"

"He will never look for you down in Hell."

"But it's *Hell!*"

"So, take a nap. Many are being dragged to Hell right now by the demons, anyway. You'd probably be dragged down there eventually, too. Maybe we can disguise you. You'd hope for Hell if you knew what my step-father would do to either of us if he finds us here."

"No," I shake my head, "I won't."

"Not a choice, Princess," he tells me.

"What? You're going to kidnap me?"

He sighs. "I'd rather not, Bella. I'd rather you come with me willingly."

I rub my forehead with my thumb and forefinger. I want to cry again.

Without another word, I go toward the bathroom. My mom has run the bath and filled it with lemon-scented Epsom salts. I undress, get in the tub, and rub the salt all over my body. What will I do? Is this all my fault? Why didn't I... couldn't I have... shouldn't I have...? I feel sick. I might puke. I scroll through my phone out of bad habit. There are hundreds of messages from Daven.

All I see are newscasts of Hell on Earth... at least, in our little town. I see Daven's father, the mayor, handing out shotguns at the Capitol. I see people being dragged under water, dragged into trees. I see blood running through the streets.

I lean over the side of the tub and puke.

When I finally managed to rub the salt into every crevice of my body, I put on the pair of pajamas that my mom gave me. They smell like laundry detergent, like home, like her. And it's all my fault that this will all be gone within a matter of days, maybe hours.

When I leave the bathroom, Draven is lying on my bed.

"I'll go with you if we can release everyone from Hell."

"What?" Draven sits up. "How?"

"I released your mother, didn't I? I can release

everyone who is being dragged down there. I can release the people who were wrongfully taken, and—"

"It's going to be a game you never win. As long as there are demons roaming Earth, you'll have to keep on releasing people over and over and over—"

"Whatever! I'll sacrifice myself. I'll make it my life's work to lead people out of the Underworld. I *am* a chosen one. This is my fault; this is my doing. I will spend an eternity correcting my mistakes. I will spend an eternity underground in torture to fix this mistake."

"Wow," Draven shakes his head, "you really are a good person. You are much better than me, and much too good for me."

"Prove me wrong," I say to him. "Help me do it."

CHAPTER 12
CECE PORTER'S POV

I don't understand what's going on, but I know everyone on TV looks scared. Everyone except mama.

She pulls me up the stairs. I'm wearing my new yellow raincoat that Daven gave to me from Bella. When he got home, mom and dad took him to bed because he got hit by a car today. That would've been the weirdest part of my day if it's not currently raining tar, if cars aren't being abandoned on the streets, if I couldn't hear the screams of the city from inside our gated home.

If I didn't know that demons are roaming the streets.

"How do you know that?" mama asks. She gives me a necklace that's decorated with pentagrams. It has one large crystal, called selenite, hanging down from the center. I put it around my neck.

"I just have a feeling," I reply. And I do. As soon as the tar began raining down, it was as sure as seeing a nest with eggs in it. Those are going to be baby birds— there are demons roaming the streets.

My mama smiles. "Your powers are strong, my love."

"Will they get us?" I ask.

She shakes her head. "Our gates are made of iron. They will never get through."

"Is the world over?"

"Not if I can help it."

Mama kisses me on the forehead and picks me up. She hasn't picked me up like this in a long time. She stands tall and strong and confident, though I'm sure there is a worry deep inside of her. But if there really is a worry, she refuses to let me know. She never does. With her, I am stronger because she is strong.

She takes me down a long hallway and brings me toward a closet. It's always been locked. Mama said her wedding China is in there. So, I don't care about it being locked, not until now. Not until she unlocks it, and I see an entire room in there. It's made of iron, with beautiful sparkling pentagrams drawn across the floor and the ceiling, with salt lining all the walls and no windows.

"What is this?" I ask.

"You stay in here, okay? I'm going to go get your brother. You will both stay in here until this all blows over."

I shake my head quickly, my pigtails bouncing. "Where will you go? Can I go with you? Where is papa?"

"He's fixing this the only way he knows how. Luckily, I know a better way."

"Can I please go with you?"

"Afraid not, sweetie." She pushes me through the door and closes it behind me.

I sigh, going toward a velvety chair near the wall. When I sit down, I feel something poke my butt. There is something sharp in the pocket of this coat. Another gift from Bella?

I pull out a large golden pentagram on a string, beaded with gorgeous crystal beads. It begins to glow in my hands.

"I better bring this to mama. This will help," I whisper to myself, easily pushing the door open and going to find her.

CHAPTER 13
BELLA NOVA'S POV

Hell wasn't packed before.

There is nothing compared to this.

When we enter Hell again, something new plays on the mirror. It's not my murder of Brick. This time, it's of me having sex with Draven. It's our relationship that plays back. He's sad next to me as he watches my greatest sin, *him*.

But I don't care anymore. I'm done with love, and

I'm done with Earthly things. I am sacrificing myself. I will help others escape from Hell.

After I view my greatest sin, I am nearly suffocated with the compaction of other humans. They are crying, asking where they are, screaming.

"How do I know who's a demon and who's human?" I ask Draven. As I open my mouth, elbows and fingers touch my tongue.

"They're all demons now."

"How am I to know who is good, and who can be released?"

"Bella!" he screams to me over the yelling. "You *won't* know. It'll be hard to know."

I encourage the people to grab onto me, first going for those I already recognize... which just happens to be Stephanie and her minions. Stephanie cries, sobs, screams, eyes bleeding as she grabs onto my neck like a child getting a piggyback ride. She is the first person I save.

"Go hide. Rub your body with Epsom salt. Draw a pentagram on yourself. Find something that smells like lemon, wear bright clothes, do what you can to think happy thoughts," I say to her. She's still crying, listening only long enough to hear the full speech, then takes off running, tripping over herself in the distance.

It's exhausting watching Draven and I over and over again, our entire relationship playing on a mirror as I go back and forth in between Hell and Earth. It's torture for Draven, too, and we take turns playing our greatest sins in the mirror for entrance into Hell as we go back and forth.

His first few times is an image of him sacrificing his own twin brother in order to meet Lucifer, to have food and money. As he watches our relationship through my eyes more, his sin eventually changes. He, too, watches the abuse that he'd put me through.

It's like feeling the pain of a breakup that should've never been a relationship in the first place, and it's agony. But if I have to spend an eternity doing this, maybe it's what I deserve.

Our fifteenth time down, Draven stops me before I go back up.

"My sister is calling for me," he says. But I don't hear anything.

"Yeah, right," I huff, someone's hair filling my mouth. "You're just sick of this. You're just being a coward."

"Come with me!" He pulls me by the hand before I can say anything else.

We move quietly through the crowd of bodies, and I see the route that he had taken me when we first saved his mother and sister. Past the bodies, there are walls of fire, and the ceiling is made of tar. He pulls it down over us, and instead of being in the tar like I had expected, we're in the empty sunset room.

On the wall of the sunset room, his sister—looking much more human-like—appears.

"I have the amulet," she says.

Draven sighs. "Great. So, that's the end, right? Of the human race?"

She shakes her head. "I have made a friend."

Behind his sister, I can make out a pair of familiar pigtails.

"CeCe?" I whisper.

"The amulet will stop the war," his sister says, "and send all the demons back to Hell, bring the dead back to life, reverse it all, and erase their memories."

"So, what are you going to do? Destroy it?"

She shakes her head. "I like it here. And I like my new friend."

"Hi, Bella!" CeCe waves. "I like your pajamas!"

I look down at my pajamas, now covered in dirt and blood.

"CeCe?" I cry out. "Are you safe?"

"I don't like her," his sister huffs. "She's hysterical. We should leave her in Hell."

"No!" CeCe yells. "I love Bella. Bring her back up here."

"I'm letting you keep the amulet and send all the demons back to Hell," Melanesia responds, turning to CeCe. "I desire one thing, and it is for her to stay down there."

My heart stops. I feel the breath leave my lungs, like it has already been decided.

If this is what I deserve, then fine.

"No," Draven interjects, "let me stay down here in her place."

"You?" His sister laughs. "My father will torture you forever. For eternity!"

Draven looks over at me, and tears fall down his face. "I will sacrifice myself. This is all my fault."

"But you just got your mother back!" I shake my head. "You just got your sister back."

He falls to his knees. "I am a monster, Bella. This is all my fault. It was my fault that she was even down here in the first place."

"Mother will want you back." Melanesia has a mischievous smile pressed across her face.

"Mother hates me," Draven mumbles. "She will want her son. She will want the son I killed. Bring him back, Melanesia. She will be happy."

"Hmm," she sings. Then she shrugs. "Okay."

"Draven, thank you—" I reach out to hold him, and he is on his knees, crying, fearful, frantic, and suddenly, I am at the creek again. The water is running over my bare feet.

CHAPTER 14
DAVEN PORTER'S POV

I don't remember anything after the car accident. I have some stitches on my head and some bruises on my ribs, but that's all. Bella comes over to my house, but not to see me. She tells me that Draven is gone, and she's almost sad about it.

And I must have a concussion because as the women whisper in the kitchen, it sounds like *CeCe* is the reason that Draven is gone.

"Your mother said the authorities might be on their

way," my mother says to Bella. "She asked me to keep you safe."

Bella sighs. "Daven, can you please give us a moment alone?"

I nod, going toward the kitchen door. But I still press my head against it and hear my mother say, "So you killed him, Bella? But he was possessed, right? And a bad man, wasn't he—Cliff!"

My dad comes down the stairs, and he also looks shaken. He looks a bit bruised, a little pale.

"Get away from that door," he says sternly. I do. I go into the living room, watching them from the frosted glass that separates the two rooms.

I can see them, blurrily, as I sit on the couch, grasping for words that they are saying. My dad comes out of the kitchen quickly and goes toward his office, and I hear Bella speaking.

"The guilt was killing me," she says, "and after everything that's happened—"

And then her voice gets quiet again. This sucks, and I'm done waiting to speak to her.

I go toward the kitchen and open the door.

"CeCe," Bella crouches down, putting her hands out toward my baby sister, "it seems I have a lot to thank you for today."

She whispers, "I saw him before. In my dreams."

"Nightmares," Bella corrects.

"Oh, no," CeCe says, looking at me, "dreams. I've killed him every time. It was... glorious!"

"Your mother never told you that you're a descendant, right?"

CeCe shakes her head.

"A descendant?" I ask. They ignore me.

"Well, I don't think I can get away from telling her," my mother chimes in.

Bella smiles, then hesitates, blushing before she asks, "Did you know right away when you met me?"

"You look just like your mother. If I had seen her in town, or known she had moved back, I'd have recognized her right away."

"I guess being a shut-in has some benefits," Bella laughs, giving a side smile, "or maybe it doesn't. Maybe this whole thing could've been avoided."

"Things always go how they should. Life isn't a fairytale, Bella." My mother winks. "Go get some rest. You two have a lot to catch up on." She then looks over at me.

Bella smiles and looks at my sister, crouching down to whisper in her ear as my mother turns on her heels to the screaming tea kettle. I can just barely hear Bella whisper, "Be careful about your new friend. Do you have the—"

And then CeCe holds up a strange golden necklace that I've never seen before.

"Trade me?" Bella asks. She gives CeCe the pentagram ring from her own finger, and Bella takes the necklace. She leaves it on the counter as my mom pours a cup of tea, and my mother puts it into her pocket quickly.

I hold my hand out to Bella, and she takes it, following me to my bedroom. When we get there, we collapse onto my bed, exhausted. Though thoughts tempt me, I'm exhausted, and I can tell she is, too.

She is wearing a pair of dirty pajamas—blue and white striped shorts and a white tank top—that she saved (or nearly ended?) the world in. There is dirt on her forehead. She has her hair, tangled and matted, in a bun at the top of her head.

"I don't think I understand what happened today." I am trying to understand what I saw, who I saw, what CeCe had to do with any of this. What my mother knows and why she knows it. All I know for certain, at this moment, is that I was right about Draven. And I'm proud of it.

"I can try to start from the beginning," she says. "Start with what happened in Oregon."

And then I remember why Bella is here in the first place, hiding out in our mansion while her family goes to find help from all corners of the world. Because there are authorities on the way, for one reason or another.

"Tell me."

"I haven't made the best decisions my whole life," she explains, tucking a strand of hair behind her ear.

If it's stupid to fall under her spell, to believe her innocence even knowing her guilt, than I am a fool. I will wear the badge with honor. I give her a kiss on the forehead and tell her I don't need any more details. I go over to my dresser, where a red bag has been waiting for her. Inside the bag is a black box. I pull out a ring, my grandmother's, from the box.

"This isn't a marriage proposal, because I think both our moms would lose their minds." I laugh. She smiles, tears filling her eyes. "But it *is* an honest promise, Bella."

She shakes her head. "I don't even know where to being, Daven. You have only been honest with me. You never faltered; you never lied. I love you, Daven, and I'm sorry for everything."

I shrug. "I could've gone about things differently, too."

She takes the ring and looks it over before putting it on her finger. "The ring of a descendant, your grandmother. Our marriage will be so blessed."

She is beaming, but then she frowns, taking the ring off her finger.

"Is there something wrong?"

She hands it back to me.

"I made some bad choices before I moved here, Daven."

I laugh. "There's nothing that could stop me from marrying you, Bella. You could've killed a man in cold blood, and I'd still love you."

Her eyes widen, and she puts her hand over her mouth. "What?"

Her voice is muffled.

"What?" I ask. I feel a little light-headed, but I think I've solved the mystery. "Did you... you didn't..."

Bella looks down at her hand, now ringless. "He

was going to hurt me, Daven. And it's complicated. It's hard to explain all these factors, but maybe one day, your mom will sit you down and—"

"I don't care."

"But if I'm arrested, if I have to go to jail... I don't think self-defense counts if you pick up and run, Daven, and I'm scared I'll have to go away—"

"No," I shake my head, "take this ring and put it on. Let me go talk to my dad—"

"Your mother has already asked him to look things over and—"

"No," I say again.

I shut the door behind me and go down the hall, toward the study.

When I look through the glass panes of his French doors, he has his reading glasses on and is peering over a paper document that's thick with length. Before I even knock, my hand hanging limp in front of the door, he motions for me to enter. I do so quietly.

"Dad, I..."

"It seems that we are harboring a fugitive," he simply says.

I can see now that the document, even with its thickness, has small letters. It seems as if a hundred paragraphs are spread across one page. When I was younger, I would be shocked with the way he reads these papers. But he always told me that it was his degree in law, his political background, that has prepared him to read these. I asked if all those in power could do what he does, and he just laughed.

He laughed because he said no one else cared enough.

"I don't think she—"

"Spare me." He puts up his hand. "I don't have time. She did it. But truth is, the man she killed was an awful man, and there's irrefutable evidence pointing to that. The biggest crime she committed wasn't the killing, but the running."

"What can you do?"

"Well," he motions toward the papers, "that is what I'm trying to figure out."

"Sir." I'm surprised to hear Bella's voice behind me. My dad looks up at her, peering just above his glasses to see her in her dirty pajamas.

"You've had quite the day, Ms. Nova," he replies. "You should be resting."

I see Bella raise an eyebrow. "You know what my day was like?"

He gives her a soft, knowing smile. "I don't remember first-hand, but my wife has filled me in on the details. It is a blessing and a curse—no, only a blessing—that you women are the only ones who will remember today. You should be *resting*. It was because you didn't rest that you made the irrational decision to confess to the crime."

"In my defense—"

"No need to defend yourself here. I think you did the right thing. It's just a matter of helping everyone else see that you did the right thing."

"And if they do, we might have a chance?"

He sighs, scratching his forehead. "Bella, why did your family run?"

She comes forward, pushing past me to sit on the chair in front of his desk. I feel invisible, as I should. Bella has seen so much. She and my father know what true pain and dedication and loyalty and sacrifice are. In this way, they are immortal. Their age isn't a number but a status, a badge they wear.

She is calm and collected, her answer clear. "If you thought Daven had done something wrong, if you were worried that bringing it into the light would be a danger to the world... wouldn't you have done the same?"

My dad thinks about this, thumb stroking his chin. "I'd love to speak to your mother and father. It must've taken a lot out of them."

"They never should've had me," she utters, and not in an angry or petty way, just a statement of fact. "But my grandmother never should've had her, and so on and so forth. They knew what our blood would bring on the day of the reckoning. But she gave birth to me and just wanted me to have a normal life. Wouldn't you just want your kids to have a normal life?"

"I do." He nods. "I always have. We went through the same thing before having Daven—I can't even tell you how many superstitions we attempted just to make sure he came out a boy. We did the same things with CeCe, and despite it all, she came out this spitfire of a girl. And thank goodness. Without her, we'd all be... well. We'll figure this out, Ms. Nova. I can make no guarantees, but I foresee my son and you having a bright future. Jail time is not in that future. Reconciliation of some sort, maybe. But not jail time."

"Thank you so much," she whispers, her voice cracking.

I'm relieved when he says it, and I can see Bella's shoulders deflate. She looks back at me, eyes widening, pleased. I am beaming at her.

"Relax, though. No wedding bells until you both graduate. Then we'll be happy to do for you what we can to make your dream wedding possible." My dad looks at me when he says this, and he winks. I look down at Bella's hand, where my grandmother's sparking ring sits in place of her pentagram ring. It looks much better, suits her so much better.

I cannot wait to put a ring on that finger and invite her to be my bride.

EPILOGUE

BELLA NOVA'S POV

Ten years later...

I cry out in the middle of the night sometimes because I hear him. I cannot, and will not, explain this ever-present connection to Daven. I don't need to, I don't think.

It's possible to hate someone, and love someone, and be thankful for them, and regret ever meeting them, all at the same time. Because that is how I feel about Draven.

On nights where I am able, if I fall asleep in just the right manner, I visit him. He isn't in as much trouble as he and his sister had imagined—his sister, who is now the "godmother" of my son, all of its irony making us laugh—and his father didn't remember anything about the great war. None of the demons did. The amulet was more powerful than anyone could've imagined. And how funny then, that I had lost it for twelve years because I had taken it and put it in my pocket.

Daven and I got married on the day my case was closed. It was a case of self-defense. I was free to live my life, and I went on to open a non-profit organization to support women who have been in similar situations.

Cliff Porter found a bunch of lawyers to support my cause, to help other women who acted in self-defense be free. What the lawyers didn't know was that about one in five clients actually killed someone they had truly loved, who had been possessed by a demon. Those were the hardest cases, but those women deserved their freedom, too.

The coven community is stronger now than it was in my mother's day. I practice, with my mother and mother-in-law, during full moons, new moons, and dark moons. We tell Daven that we're just going to brunch and the mall. Melanesia and her mother even come every now and then, though her mother tries to stay away from all that stuff. She'll come around, though.

I am pregnant. Today, we find out the gender. She is a girl. She is a new descendant. And it is time that we tell Daven the truth.

UNLEASHING HELL BOOK THREE

SAVING THEM

VIOLA TEMPEST

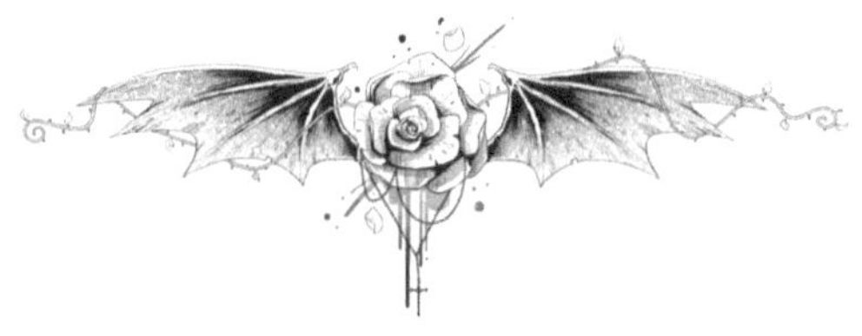